A BRIEF INTRODUCTION TO THE INFINITESIMAL CALCULUS

MAVEN BOOKS

A BRIEF INTRODUCTION TO THE INFINITESIMAL CALCULUS

IRVING FISHER

Professor of Political Economy In Yale University,
Co-Author of Phillip's and Fisher's "Elements of Geometry"

MAVEN BOOKS

Chennai   Trichy   New Delhi

MAVEN BOOKS

This edition has been published in india by arrangement with Carson Books, UK

ISBN 978-93-5527-064-1   Maven Books

All rights reserved   No. 44, Nallathambi Street,
Printed and bound in India   Triplicane, Chennai 600 005

MJP 1216   © Publishers, 2023

Publisher :   C. Janarthanan

Publisher's Note

The legacy of a country is in its varied cultural heritage, historical literature, developments in the field of economy and science. The top nations in the world are competing in the field of science, economy and literature. This vast legacy has to be conserved and documented so that it can be bestowed to the future generation. The knowledge of this legacy is slowly getting perished in the present generation due to lack of documentation.

Keeping this in mind, the concern with retrospective acquiring of rare books has been accented recently by the burgeoning reprint industry. Maven Books is gratified to retrieve the rare collections with a view to bring back those books that were landmarks in their time.

In this effort, a series of rare books would be republished under the banner, "Maven Books". The books in the reprint series have been carefully selected for their contemporary usefulness as well as their historical importance within the intellectual. We reconstruct the book with slight enhancements made for better presentation, without affecting the contents of the original edition.

Most of the works selected for republishing covers a huge range of subjects, from history to anthropology. We believe this reprint edition will be a service to the numerous researchers and practitioners active in this fascinating field. We allow readers to experience the wonder of peering into a scholarly work of the highest order and seminal significance.

MAVEN BOOKS

PREFACE

THIS little volume contains the substance of lectures by which I have been accustomed to introduce the more advanced of my students to a course in modern economic theory. I could find no text-book sufficiently brief for my purpose, nor one which distributed the emphasis in the desired manner. My object, however, in preparing my notes for publication has not been principally to provide a book for classroom use. It must be admitted that very few teachers of Economics as yet desire to address their students in the mathematical tongue. I have had in mind not so much the classroom as the study. Teachers and students alike, however little they care about the mathematical medium for their own ideas, are growing to feel the need of it in order to understand the ideas of others. I have frequently received inquiries, as doubtless have other teachers, for some book which would enable a person without special mathematical training or aptitude to understand the works of Jevons, Walras, Marshall, or Pareto, or the mathematical articles constantly appearing in the *Economic Journal,* the *Journal of the Royal Statistical Society,* the *Giornale degli Economisti,* and elsewhere. It is such a book that I have tried to write.

The immediate occasion for its publication is the appearance in English of Cournot's *Principes mathématiques de la théorie des richesses*, in Professor Ashley's series of " Economic Classics." The " non-mathematical " reader can only expect to understand the general trend of reasoning in this masterly little memoir. If he finds it as stimulating as most readers have, he will want to comprehend its notation and processes in detail.

I have tried in some measure to meet the varying needs of different readers by using two sorts of type. If desired, most of the fine print may be omitted on first reading, and all on second. The reader is, however, advised not to pass over all of the examples.

Although intended primarily for economic students, the book is equally adapted to the use of those who wish a short course in " The *C*alculus " as a matter of general education. I therefore venture the hope that teachers of mathematics may find it useful as a text-book in courses planned especially for the " general student." I have long been of the opinion that the fundamental conceptions and processes of the Infinitesimal Calculus are of greater educational value than those of Analytical Geometry or Trigonometry, which at present find a conspicuous place in our school and college curricula. Moreover, they are almost as easily learned, and far less easily forgotten.

IRVING. FISHER.

New Haven, September, 1897.

PREFACE TO THE THIRD EDITION

In the present edition have been incorporated several changes and additions originally prepared for the German translation of 1904 and for a Japanese translation in preparation.

A preliminary statement of the concepts of limits and several new examples have also been inserted.

IRVING FISHER.

November, 1905.

CONTENTS

	PAGE
INTRODUCTION	xi

CHAPTER I

THE GENERAL METHOD OF DIFFERENTIATION 1

CHAPTER II

GENERAL THEOREMS OF DIFFERENTIATION 16

CHAPTER III

DIFFERENTIATION OF THE ELEMENTARY FUNCTIONS . . . 30

CHAPTER IV

SUCCESSIVE DIFFERENTIATION — MAXIMA AND MINIMA . . 37

CHAPTER V

TAYLOR'S THEOREM 49

CHAPTER VI

INTEGRAL CALCULUS 57

APPENDIX

FUNCTIONS OF MORE THAN ONE VARIABLE 73

INTRODUCTION

THE reader of the following book should be familiar with ordinary algebraic operations and with the concepts of variation and limits, a brief statement of which is here appended.

Continuous Variation.—Suppose the line ab to represent all possible magnitudes between $-a$ and $+b$; suppose om to represent one magnitude between $-a$ and $+b$; this magnitude is said to *vary continuously* when it increases or

$$-a \qquad\qquad o \qquad m \qquad m_1 \quad m_2 \quad m_3 \qquad +b$$

FIG. I.

decreases in such a manner that m may occupy any position whatever between $-a$ and $+b$.

Limits.—If we conceive om to have an infinite succession of magnitudes such that m may occupy the positions m_1, m_2, m_3, etc., making the *ultimate* difference between ob and om less than any assignable positive quantity, then om is a *variable* and ob is its *limit.*

It is clear, then, that the difference between the limit ob and the variable om is *another variable magnitude* whose limit is zero. A variable, with a limit zero, is called an *infinitesimal.*

xi

Application to Infinite Series. — In a converging infinite series, the sum of each successive term and those preceding approaches a magnitude understood to be designated by the series. This magnitude is called the 'sum' of the series.

Thus, the repeating decimal .666 ⋯,

or, $$\frac{6}{10}+\frac{6}{10^2}+\frac{6}{10^3}+\frac{6}{10^4}+\cdots,$$

means a series of successive magnitudes, viz.:

(*a*) $\dfrac{6}{10}$, which is less than $\frac{2}{3}$.

(*b*) $\dfrac{6}{10}+\dfrac{6}{10^2}$, which is less than $\frac{2}{3}$, but more nearly approximates $\frac{2}{3}$ than (*a*).

(*c*) $\dfrac{6}{10}+\dfrac{6}{10^2}+\dfrac{6}{10^3}$, which is less than $\frac{2}{3}$, but more nearly approximates $\frac{2}{3}$ than (*b*).

(*d*) $\dfrac{6}{10}+\dfrac{6}{10^2}+\dfrac{6}{10^3}+\dfrac{6}{10^4}$, which is less than $\frac{2}{3}$, but more nearly approximates $\frac{2}{3}$ than (*c*).

Thus, as the number of terms of the series is increased, the sum of the terms remains always less than $\frac{2}{3}$, but approximates ultimately as nearly $\frac{2}{3}$ as may be desired, *i.e.* converges towards $\frac{2}{3}$. We therefore, by convention, speak of $\frac{2}{3}$ as the 'sum,' or limit, of this infinite series.

THEOREMS.

1. *The limit of the sum of two different variables (which approach limits) is the sum of the limits of those variables.*

2. *The limit of the difference of two different variables (which approach limits) is the difference of the limits of those variables.*

3. *The limit of the product of two different variables (which approach limits) is the product of the limits of those variables.*

4. *The limit of the quotient of two different variables (which approach limits) is the quotient of the limits of those variables.*

INFINITESIMAL CALCULUS

⸻ ∘∘⟩⟨∘∘ ⸻

CHAPTER I

THE GENERAL METHOD OF DIFFERENTIATION

1. The Infinitesimal Calculus treats of the ultimate ratios of vanishing quantities. This definition, however, can only become intelligible after some actual acquaintance with " ultimate ratios."

2. The conception of a limiting or ultimate ratio is fundamental in many familiar relations. It is impossible, without it, to obtain a clear notion of what is the *velocity* of a body *at an instant.* The *average* velocity of the body during a *period* of time may readily be defined as the quotient of the space traversed during that period divided by the time of traversing it. If a steamer crosses the Atlantic (3000 miles) in 6 days, we may say that the *average* speed is 3000 ÷ 6, or 500, miles per day. But this does not tell us the speed at various points in the voyage, under head winds, storms, or other conditions, favorable or unfavorable. What, for instance, was the speed at noon of the third day out? We may obtain a first approximation to the desired result by taking the average speed for a short time after the given instant; that is, taking the ratio of the distance traversed during (say) the following hour to the time of traversing it, which is $\frac{1}{24}$ of a day. If this distance be 20 miles, we obtain $20 \div \frac{1}{24}$, or 480 miles per day, as the average speed *during that hour*. For a second approximation we take a minute instead of an hour; for a third, a second instead of a minute, and so on. The ratio of the space traversed to the time of traversing it becomes closer and closer to the true speed. Though both the time and space approach zero as limit, their *ratio* does not. The limit which this *ratio* approaches, or the *ultimate* ratio of the distance traversed to the time of traversing it when both distance and time vanish, is the precise speed *at the instant*.

3. Let us apply this method of obtaining velocity to bodies falling in a vacuum. We know from experience that the distance fallen equals sixteen times the square of the time of falling, *i.e.* $s = 16\,t^2$, where s is the distance fallen from rest (measured in feet), and t is the time of falling (in seconds). Consider the body at some particular instant, t being the time to this particular point and s the distance. Suppose we wait until the time has increased by a small increment Δt, during which the body increases its distance from the starting-point, s, by the small increment Δs. Since the above formula holds true of *all* points, it holds true now, when the time is $t + \Delta t$, and the distance is $s + \Delta s$. That is,

$$s + \Delta s = 16\,(t + \Delta t)^2.$$

This gives

$$s + \Delta s = 16\,t^2 + 32\,t \cdot \Delta t + 16(\Delta t)^2.$$

But

$$s \quad\;\; = 16\,t^2.$$

Subtracting, we have

$$\Delta s = 32\,t \cdot \Delta t + 16(\Delta t)^2,$$

whence
$$\frac{\Delta s}{\Delta t} = 32\,t + 16\,\Delta t. \tag{1}$$

This is the *average* velocity during the small interval Δt.

Thus, if $\Delta t = \frac{1}{2}$ second and t be 5 seconds, the average speed of the body during that half second (viz., the one beginning 5 seconds from rest) is $32 \times 5 + 16 \times \frac{1}{2}$, or 168 feet per second. If we take $\frac{1}{160}$ of a second instead of $\frac{1}{2}$, we have $32 \times 5 + 16 \times \frac{1}{160}$, or 160.1 feet per second.

Thus, by taking Δt smaller and smaller, we obtain the average velocity $\dfrac{\Delta s}{\Delta t}$ for a smaller and smaller interval of time immediately after the completion of the fifth second. The *limit* which $\dfrac{\Delta s}{\Delta t}$ approaches, as Δt approaches zero as its limit, is called the velocity at the very *instant* of completing the fifth second.

Its value is exactly 160, as is evident from the right-hand member of equation (1), which approaches as its limit (as t is 5 and Δt approaches zero),

$$32 \times 5 + 16 \times 0, \text{ or } 160.$$

In general, to express the limit of both sides of equation (1) when Δt approaches zero, we write

$$\lim \frac{\Delta s}{\Delta t} = 32\,t.$$

4. The student will observe that, as Δt approaches zero, Δs also approaches zero, since a body cannot pass over any distance in no time. He must be warned, however, against expressing the limit of $\dfrac{\Delta s}{\Delta t}$ by $\dfrac{0}{0}$, which, of course, is quite indeterminate.

But in spite of the fact that the *ratio* of these *limits* of Δs and Δt is indeterminate, the *limit* of the *ratio* of Δs and Δt

may be entirely determinate. It is only with this latter conception, viz. the limit of $\frac{\Delta s}{\Delta t}$, or $\lim \frac{\Delta s}{\Delta t}$, that the student has to deal.

The limit of the ratio of the vanishing quantities Δs and Δt, or $\lim \frac{\Delta s}{\Delta t}$, is called the "*derivative*" of s with respect to t; because, from $s = 16\,t^2$ we *derive* $\lim \frac{\Delta s}{\Delta t} = 32\,t$.

In fact, we may speak of either member of the latter of these two equations as the *derivative* of either member of the former equation. For instance, $32\,t$ is the derivative of $16\,t^2$.

5. Other names and notations are also used. Thus instead of $\lim \frac{\Delta s}{\Delta t}$ it is usual to employ the shorter symbol $\frac{ds}{dt}$. In this expression ds and dt are called *differentials* of s and t, just as Δs and Δt are called *increments* of s and t. But they are not zeros. They have no definite value individually. We may select any value we please for one of them. But when this one is fixed, the other is also, since the two must be kept in a ratio equal to $\lim \frac{\Delta s}{\Delta t}$. We say therefore that the differentials ds and dt are any two quantities which bear to each other the ratio which is the limit of the ratio between Δs and Δt.

Other names for $\lim \frac{\Delta s}{\Delta t}$ or $\frac{ds}{dt}$, besides "derivative," are "differential quotient" and "differential coefficient."

6. In the particular case considered above, the differential quotient is a velocity and may be denoted by v. Equation (2) thus becomes * $v = 32\,t$.

---

* If distance be measured in centimetres instead of in feet, we should have $v = 980\,t$, and in general $v = gt$, where g is a constant depending for its numerical value on the units chosen for measuring space and time.

Velocity at a point may now be defined as *the ultimate ratio of the space traversed just after passing the point to the time of traversing it when the space and time approach zero as limit.*

7. EXAMPLES.

1. What is the velocity of a body which has fallen 10 seconds? 100 seconds? $1\frac{1}{2}$ seconds?

2. What is the velocity of a body which has fallen 16 feet?

HINT. — First find how many seconds it has fallen by using $s = 16\,t^2$.

3. What is the velocity of a body which has fallen 64 feet? 4 feet? 1 foot? 2 feet?

4. It being known that a body, falling not from rest, but with an initial velocity of 5 feet per second, obeys the law

$$s = 16\,t^2 + 5\,t, \tag{1}$$

what will be its velocity at the end of any time t?

HINT. — Let t receive an increment Δt, causing s to increase by Δs, so that

$$s + \Delta s = 16(t + \Delta t)^2 + 5(t + \Delta t). \tag{2}$$

Subtract (1) from (2), divide by Δt and then reduce Δt and Δs to zero.

$$Ans.\ \lim \frac{\Delta s}{\Delta t} = 32\,t + 5.$$

5. What will be the velocity at the end of 10 seconds? At the end of 69 feet?

6. It being known that a body falling with an initial velocity of u obeys the law $s = \frac{1}{2}g t^2 + u t$, what will be its velocity at the end of time t? When $t = 3$?

8. When one quantity *depends* upon another, the first is said to be a *function* of the second. A change in the second is in general *accompanied by* a change in the first. In each case the limits, within which the function relation exists should be specified.

Thus the distance a body falls from rest is a function of the time of falling, for how far the body falls depends on how long it has fallen; · the demand for an article is a function of its price, for if the price changes the demand changes; if $y = x^2$, then y is a function of x, for a variation in the magnitude of x necessitates also a variation in the magnitude of y.

9. When one quantity is a function of another, the latter is called the *independent variable*, and the former the *dependent variable*.

The distinction between the independent and the dependent variable is only for convenience of expression. The two may be interchanged.

Thus, as the distance of a falling body from the starting-point changes, there is also a change in the time it has taken. Hence we may say that " time of falling " is a function of " distance fallen." Similarly price may be regarded as a function of demand. Again, $y = x^2$ may be written $x = \sqrt{y}$, thus making x a function of y. The idea of functional dependence is therefore quite different from that of *causal* dependence. Functional dependence is a *mutual* relation.

In the example of falling bodies s was a function of t, and what we accomplished was to find the differential quotient or derivative of that function. The derivative in this case was a *velocity*. In general the process of finding the differential quotient of any given function is called *differentiation*, and is the subject matter of the *Differential* Calculus, one of the two branches into which the Infinitesimal Calculus is divided. The Differential Calculus will occupy us in the first five chapters of this book.

10. A second important application of the idea of a differential quotient of a function is to the *tangential direction* of a curve at any point on it. The Calculus enables us to conceive in the most general manner of a tangent to a curve. The student should observe that the usual definition of a tangent to a circle will not apply to any and all curves. A straight line may have only one point in common with a curve and yet cut it and not be tangent.

11. Let RS be a curve whose equation is

$$y = 1 + 5x - x^2. \tag{1}$$

That is, for *any* point P upon it, the "ordinate," y (or distance, PA, from that point to the horizontal axis), is related

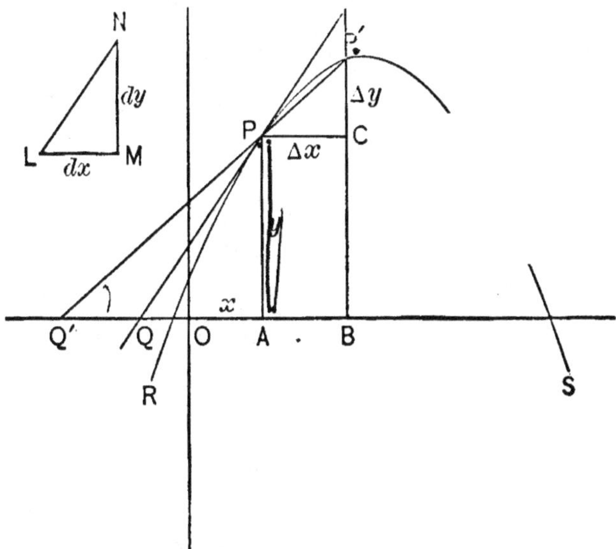

Fig. 1.

to the "abscissa," x (or distance, OA, from the vertical axis), in the manner expressed by (1). PA is a function of OA; *i.e.* the height, PA, of *any* point P on the curve depends upon its distance, OA, from the vertical axis.

What is the direction of the curve at the point P? The direction from the point P to another point P' is the direction of the secant line $Q'PP'$. The point P' has for abscissa,

$x + \Delta x$, and for ordinate, $y + \Delta y$. Since the relation (1) holds true of all points on the curve, it holds true of P'.

Hence $\qquad y + \Delta y = 1 + 5(x + \Delta x) - (x + \Delta x)^2,$

or $\qquad y + \Delta y = 1 + 5x + 5\Delta x - x^2 - 2x\Delta x - (\Delta x)^2.$

Subtracting $\qquad y = 1 + 5x - x^2,$

we have $\qquad \Delta y = 5\Delta x - 2x\Delta x - (\Delta x)^2,$

whence $\qquad \dfrac{\Delta y}{\Delta x} = 5 - 2x - \Delta x.$

We may pause here a·moment to see what this result means. $\dfrac{\Delta y}{\Delta x}$ or $\dfrac{P'C}{PC}$ is the "slope" of the line $Q'PP'$. That is, it is the rate at which a point moving from Q' toward P' rises in proportion to its horizontal progress. It is the same sort of magnitude as that referred to as the "grade" of an uphill road which rises "so many feet to the mile (horizontally)." If $\dfrac{\Delta y}{\Delta x} = \dfrac{1}{10}$, $Q'PP'$ rises one foot in every ten horizontally. The "slope" of a line shows its direction.

The equation $\dfrac{\Delta y}{\Delta x} = 5 - 2x - \Delta x$ shows that the "slope" of the secant line $Q'PP'$ is to be found by taking 5 and subtracting, first, two times the number of units in OA and then the number of units in AB. For instance, if $OA = 2$ and $AB = \frac{1}{2}$, then

$$\frac{\Delta y}{\Delta x} = 5 - 2 \times 2 - \tfrac{1}{2} = \tfrac{1}{2};$$

i.e. the secant slopes 1 foot up for every 2 feet sidewise.

12. But we have not yet reached the tangent at P. Let the point P' be gradually shifted along the curve toward P until it ultimately coincides. The secant $Q'P'$ will gradually change its direction and approach a limiting position QP. This *limiting position* we call the tangent.   Its slope is

$$\frac{dy}{dx} = 5 - 2x.$$

Thus, if x (i.e. OA) is 2, $\frac{dy}{dx} = 1$.   That is, QP is inclined at $45°$. If x is 4, $\frac{dy}{dx} = -3$; *i.e.* the curve slopes *down*, not up.

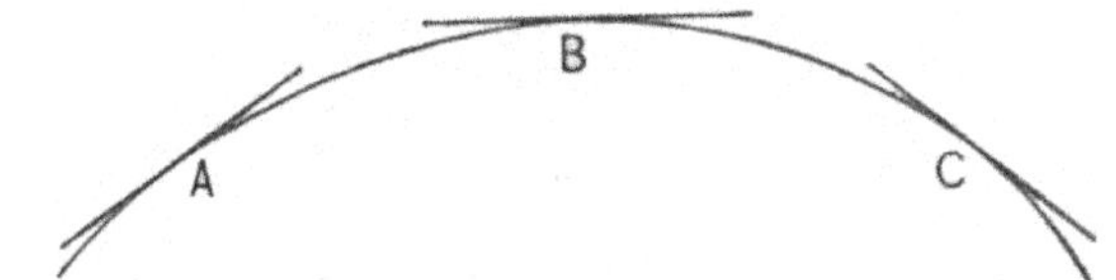

FIG. 2. -- A, positive slope; B, zero slope; C, negative slope.

EXAMPLES.

1. What is the slope of the tangent to the above curve at the point whose abscissa is 1 ? 0 ? $2\frac{1}{2}$? What does the answer to the last mean ? 3 ? What does this mean ? 6 ? -1 ?

2. Derive the formula for the slope of the tangent to the curve $y = 1 + x + x^2$.

13. To construct a tangent at P, all we need to do is to draw a line through P with the required slope.   Thus, if we wish the tangent to the point whose abscissa is 1, we find from the above formula that its slope is 3.   We therefore lay off a horizontal line LM (Fig. 1) equal to any length dx, and at its extremity erect a vertical, MN, equal to three times as much, or dy.   Draw LN; this has the required direction. Then through P draw a line parallel to LN.   This will be the tangent.

We may also call PC, dx and $P''C$, dy; for, by Sec. 5, dx and dy are simply **any two** magnitudes having a ratio equal to the limit of $\frac{\Delta y}{\Delta x}$ when Δx approaches zero as its limit.

The problem of drawing a tangent and calculating its slope was one

14. It is evident that we could approach P from the left as well as from the right. We should, however, reach the same limiting position unless there should be an angle in the curve at the point P as in Fig. 3. In this case, the progressive (PK) and regressive (HP) tangents do not coincide.

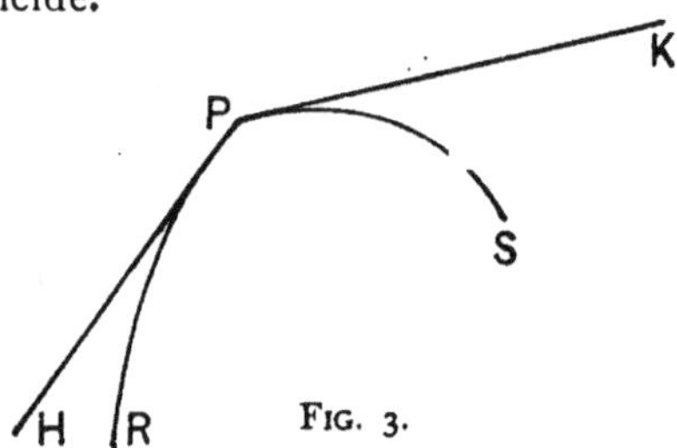

Fig. 3.

Such peculiar points are not considered in this little treatise. All the functions are such that, for the values of the independent variable which are considered, the progressive and regressive derivatives are identical. The curves considered are all "smooth," that is, bave no angles or sudden changes in direction. In many applications of the Calculus, such as to statistical or economic diagrams, it is often convenient first to smooth out the curves considered. When we want to see from a plot of the population what is the general rate of increase, we draw a tangent not to the plot of the *actual* figures, but to a *smooth curve* coinciding as nearly as possible with the plot.

The student will be able to satisfy himself in every particular case to be considered that the progressive and regressive derivatives are identical.

Thus, for $s = 16\,t^2$ in section 3, let t receive a *decrement* $\Delta't$, causing s to have a decrement $\Delta's$. Then

$$s - \Delta's = 16(t - \Delta't)^2.$$

Expanding, subtracting, and dividing as before, we obtain

$$\frac{\Delta's}{\Delta't} = 32\,t - 16\,\Delta't,$$

which reduces at the limit to

$$\frac{d's}{d't} = 32\,t, \text{ as before.}$$

Indeed, we assume in general, that it is physically impossible for a body to change its velocity *per saltum.* Hence the definition of velocity given in section 6 is equivalent to the following alternative definition : the ultimate ratio of the space traversed just *before* reaching the point to the time of traversing it when the space and time approach zero as limit.

We shall, therefore, henceforth treat only of functions whose derivatives are continuous and which are themselves continuous, within the limits considered, that is, which in changing from one value to another, pass continuously through all intermediate values.

15. We have seen that the conception of an ultimate ratio clears up the notion of velocity in mechanics and tangential slope in geometry. It is also applicable to much else in both these sciences as well as in all mathematical sciences. Momentum, acceleration, force, horsepower, density, curvature, marginal utility, marginal cost, elasticity of demand, birth rate, " force of mortality," are all examples.

The conception of an ultimate ratio or of the derivative of a function is not dependent, however, on any special application. It is purely an abstract idea of number.

16. Thus let two variables x and y fulfil the equation

$$y = x^n,$$

where n is a constant and a positive integer. We may obtain the differential quotient $\dfrac{dy}{dx}$ for any particular value of x, as follows :

Let x receive an increment Δx producing an increment of y denoted by Δy. Then, by the binomial theorem,

$$y + \Delta y = (x + \Delta x)^n,$$

$$= x^n + nx^{n-1}\Delta x + \frac{n(n-1)}{2}x^{n-2}(\Delta x)^2$$

$$+ \cdots + (\Delta x)^n$$

$$= x^n + nx^{n-1}\Delta x + \Delta x^2(\cdots).$$

Subtracting. $\quad\quad\quad y = x^n,$

we have $\quad\quad\quad\quad \Delta y = nx^{n-1}\Delta x + (\Delta x)^2(\cdots).$

Whence $\quad\quad\quad\quad \dfrac{\Delta y}{\Delta x} = nx^{n-1} + \Delta x\,(\cdots),$

where the parenthesis is evidently a finite quantity and remains finite after Δx becomes zero. Hence, when Δx becomes zero, the term $\Delta x\,(\cdots)$ becomes zero, and the equation becomes,

$$\frac{dy}{dx} = nx^{n-1}.$$

17. This is the first and most important specific formula which we have reached for the derivative of a function. It states that, to obtain the derivative of x^n, a power of x, we need only reduce the exponent by unity and use the old exponent for coefficient.

Thus the derivative of x^3 is $3x^2$. When x passes through the value 2, $3x^2$ becomes 12; that is, y, or x^3, is increasing 12 times as fast as x. $\dfrac{dy}{dx}$ is the rate at which y increases compared with the rate we make x increase. If y denotes the distance of a moving body from the starting-point, and x denotes the time it has moved, $\dfrac{dy}{dx}$, or $3x^2$, expresses its *velocity*. Again, if x and y are the "coördinates" (*i.e.* the "abscissa" and "ordinate") of a curve whose equation is $y = x^3$, then $3x^2$ is its *slope* at the point whose abscissa is x.

Although it is logically unnecessary, it is practically helpful to picture the differential quotient as a possible *velocity* or a possible *slope*. Of the two independent discoverers of the Calculus, Newton seemed to have employed the former image, and Leibnitz the latter. Newton's term for a differential quotient was " fluxion."

EXAMPLES. — **1.** Find the derivatives of x^{12}, x^5, x^2, x. What is the meaning of the answer to the last?

2. How many times as fast does y increase as x when $y = x^4$ and x is 2?

3. How fast does x^6 increase compared with x when x is -1? What does the negative answer mean?

18. The process employed in this chapter for obtaining the derivative of a function is called the "general method of differentiation." It consists (1) in giving to the independent variable a small increment, thus causing another small increment* in the dependent variable or function; (2) in writing the relation between the two variables first without and then with these increments and subtracting the first from the second; (3) in dividing through by the increment of the independent variable; (4) in passing over from $\dfrac{\Delta y}{\Delta x}$ to $\dfrac{dy}{dx}$.

This process should be thoroughly mastered by the student, for it contains, in embryo, the whole of the Infinitesimal *C*alculus.

He will observe that the order of steps (3) and (4) cannot be inverted without producing the barren result $0 = 0$.

19. Nevertheless, we can *anticipate* the result of step (4) without changing from the form of (2). Thus, the equation

$$y = 5 + 2x + 3x^2 + 5x^3$$

yields at step (2):

$$\Delta y = 2\,\Delta x + 6x\,\Delta x + 3(\Delta x)^2 + 15x^2\,\Delta x + 15x(\Delta x)^2 + 5(\Delta x)^3$$
$$= (2 + 6x + 15x^2)\,\Delta x + (3 + 15x)(\Delta x)^2 + 5(\Delta x)^3.$$

It can readily be foreseen that step (3) (*i.e.* dividing by Δx) will remove the first Δx, and reduce the exponents of the powers of Δx by one, and that therefore when step (4) is performed (*i.e.* reducing Δx to zero), all terms beyond the first will disappear, leaving $2 + 6x + 15x^2$ as the derivative. Now it is clear that this result could have been anticipated simply by *neglecting the terms involving powers*

* Decrements may always be regarded as negative increments.

of Δx higher than the first, and taking the coefficient of the first power as the required derivative.

Though this process of neglecting certain terms at step (2) is a mere anticipation of what must necessarily happen at step (4), it may be shown to be perfectly natural *in situ.* If Δx be less than one, $(\Delta x)^2$ will be less than Δx, and $(\Delta x)^3$ less than $(\Delta x)^2$, etc. By making Δx smaller and smaller, the higher powers $(\Delta x)^2$, $(\Delta x)^3$, etc., can be made indefinitely small, not only absolutely, but *in comparison with Δx.* The higher powers of Δx thus growing negligible relatively to Δx, the terms in which those powers occur as factors must also grow negligible (provided, of course, the *other* factor composing each such term does not approach infinity as limit).

Thus, if Δx is $\frac{1}{100}$, $(\Delta x)^2$ is $\frac{1}{10000}$, and $(\Delta x)^3$ only $\frac{1}{1000000}$. Consequently in the equation

$$\Delta y = (2 + 6x + 15x^2)\Delta x + (3 + 15x)(\Delta x)^2 + 5(\Delta x)^3,$$

we can, by reducing Δx sufficiently, make the terms beyond the first as small as we please *compared with the first,* no matter what be the value of x, so long as it is finite, thus keeping the parentheses finite. For instance, if x be 2, we have $\Delta y = 74\Delta x + 33(\Delta x)^2 + 5(\Delta x)^3$.

Then, if

Δx be .01, this becomes

$$\Delta y = .74 + .0033 + .000,005.$$

If $\Delta x = .001$, it becomes

$$\Delta y = .074 + .000,033 + .000,000,005.$$

If $\Delta x = .000,001$, it becomes

$$\Delta y = .000,074 + .000,000,000,033 + .000,000,000,000,000,005,$$

and the smaller we make Δx, the more negligible become the terms involving $(\Delta x)^2$ and $(\Delta x)^3$, until at the limit they become, not simply negligible " for practical purposes," but *absolutely* negligible.

The anticipatory neglect of terms involving powers of Δx higher than the first often saves a great deal of labor.

EXAMPLES.

1. Find $\dfrac{dy}{dx}$ when $y = x^5$.

2. Find $\dfrac{dy}{dx}$ when $y = x^7 + 8\,x^6 + 4$.

3. Find $\dfrac{dy}{dx}$ when $y = 10\,x^{100}$.

4. Find $\dfrac{dy}{dx}$ when $y = ax^m + bx^n$, m and n being constant and integral.   *Ans.* $amx^{m-1} + bnx^{n-1}$.

5. If x, the side of a square, has an increment i, what will be the increment of the area of the square ?

6. In the function $y = 3\,x^2 + 2\,x$, find the value of x when y increases 20 times as fast as x.   *Ans.* $x = 3$.

Differentiate the following functions:

7. $y = 3\,ab^2x^6 + c$.

8. $y = 4\,x^5 - 7\,x^3 + 2\,x - 2\,a$.   *Ans.* $20\,x^4 - 21\,x^2 + 2$.

9. $y = \tfrac{5}{3}\,x^3 - (a + b)x$.

10. $y = (b + x)^3 - bx^2$.   *Ans.* $3\,b^2 + 4\,bx + 3\,x^2$.

CHAPTER II

GENERAL THEOREMS OF DIFFERENTIATION

20. If we differentiate

$$y = 2\,x$$

by the general method, we obtain

$$\frac{dy}{dx} = 2. \tag{1}$$

Clearing this equation of fractions, we have

$$dy = 2\,dx. \tag{2}$$

This last equation is simply another form of the first, and more convenient for some purposes.

Thus, *$dy = 6\,xdx$ is a transformation of*

$$\frac{dy}{dx} = 6\,x,$$

which in turn means $\qquad \lim \frac{\Delta y}{\Delta x} = 6\,x.$

$6\,x$ is a *differential quotient* and $6\,xdx$ is a *differential*.

These conceptions are strictly correlative. To obtain the differential quotient from the differential, we simply divide by dx; to obtain the reverse, we multiply by dx.

EXAMPLES.

1. What is the differential of x^5?

2. The differential quotients of x^7, x^{10}, x^4?

21. To express the mere fact that y is a function of x, without specifying exactly *what* function, it is customary to use the letters F, f ϕ, ψ (and rarely others) followed by x in a parenthesis. They may be regarded simply as abbreviations of the word " function." Thus

$$y = \text{Function of } x$$

is abbreviated to $\qquad y = F(x).$

It is to be observed that the letters F, f, ϕ, ψ, etc., do not represent quantities like x and y, but, like Δ and d, represent *operations* on quantities.

22. The general expression for a function, such as $\phi(x)$, is often used to express, within brief compass, any *special* function. Thus if we have the equation

$$y = \frac{1 + x - 6x^5 + \dfrac{1}{ax^n}}{\dfrac{5x}{1 + x^2} + \dfrac{2 - x^3}{4x^2}},$$

we may shorten this to $y = \phi(x)$ by denoting the clumsy right-hand member by $\phi(x)$.

Again, if we have a definite curve, such as a statistical diagram, whose coördinates we call x and y, we may use

$$y = f(x)$$

to express the fact that y is related to x in the particular manner delineated by the curve.

23. The differential quotient, or derivative of a function of x, is itself a function of x.

To denote the differential quotient of

$$F(x),$$

we use the expression $\qquad F'(x)$.

Thus let $\phi(x)$ stand for x^6.
Then $\phi'(x)$ stands for $6x^5$.

The *differential* of $F(x)$ is therefore expressed by

$$F'(x)\,dx.$$

24. Another method of expressing the differential quotient of

$$F(x)$$

connects it with the general method of differentiation. Thus, if x receives an increment Δx, $F(x)$ will become

$$F(x + \Delta x).$$

This differs from its original value $F(x)$ by

$$F(x + \Delta x) - F(x).$$

The ratio of this increment of the function to the increment Δx, of the independent variable x, is

$$\frac{F(x + \Delta x) - F(x)}{\Delta x}.$$

Its limit, viz. $\qquad \lim \dfrac{F(x + \Delta x) - F(x)}{\Delta x},$

is the differential quotient of $F(x)$; *i.e.* is

$$F'(x).$$

The above process is identical with the general method of differentiation, though we have expressed it without the use of y. We might have proceeded as follows:

Put $F(x)$ equal to y so that

$$y = F(x).$$

Subtract this from $\qquad y + \Delta y = F(x + \Delta x),$

and divide by Δx, giving

$$\frac{\Delta y}{\Delta x} = \frac{F(x + \Delta x) - F(x)}{\Delta x},$$

or, at the limit

$$\frac{dy}{dx} = \lim \frac{F(x + \Delta x) - F(x)}{\Delta x}.$$

25. Yet one more notation should be familiarized. Rather it is a new application of an old one. Instead of writing $\dfrac{dy}{dx}$, we may replace y in this expression by $F(x)$, so that it reads

$$\frac{d\,[F(x)]}{dx}.$$

The student will do well now to release his mind from y as any necessary element in the analysis. It is to be regarded merely as a further abbreviation of $F(x)$.

$F(x)$ rather than y is to be thought of as primarily the function of (x). Thus, in our introductory example, instead of denoting space by s and writing $s = 16\,t^2$, we need only say if t denotes time, the function of t, $16\,t^2$, will denote space.

So also if x denotes the abscissa of a curve, $F(x)$ instead of y denotes its ordinate.

Thus, $\qquad\qquad \dfrac{d\,(x^2)}{dx}$ is $2\,x$,

or $\qquad\qquad d\,(x^2) = 2\,x dx.$

EXAMPLES. — $\qquad \dfrac{d\,(x^3)}{dx} = ? \qquad d\,(x^4) = ?$

We thus have five methods of denoting the differential quotient of y, or its equal $F(x)$; viz.:

$$\lim \frac{\Delta y}{\Delta x}, \quad \frac{dy}{dx}, \quad \frac{d\,[F(x)]}{dx}, \quad F'(x), \quad \lim \frac{F(x + \Delta x) - F(x)}{\Delta x}.$$

26. If a function of x is the sum of several functions of x, *i.e.* if

$$F(x) = f_1(x) + f_2(x) + \cdots,$$

then, since this equation holds true of all values of x, it holds true when x becomes $x + \Delta x$, so that

$$F(x + \Delta x) = f_1(x + \Delta x) + f_2(x + \Delta x) + \cdots.$$

Subtracting the upper equation from the lower, and dividing by Δx, we obtain

$$\frac{F(x + \Delta x) - F(x)}{\Delta x} = \frac{f_1(x + \Delta x) - f_1(x)}{\Delta x}$$
$$+ \frac{f_2(x + \Delta x) - f_2(x)}{\Delta x} + \cdots.$$

Now let Δx approach zero as its limit. Then for the limits of the terms in the above equation, we have:

$$\lim \frac{F(x + \Delta x) - F(x)}{\Delta x} = \lim \frac{f_1(x + \Delta x) - f_1(x)}{\Delta x} +, \text{ etc.}$$

or
$$F'(x) = f_1'(x) + f_2'(x) +, \text{ etc.}$$

That is, *the differential quotient of the sum of several func-tions is the sum of the differential quotients of those functions.* The same reasoning establishes the corresponding theorem for the *difference* of functions.

Thus the differential quotient of $x^2 + x^3$ is $2x + 3x^2$.

Sometimes the theorem is used in the differential form

$$F'(x)dx = f_1'(x)dx + f_2'(x)dx + \cdots,$$

or again
$$F'(x)dx = [f_1'(x) + f_2'(x) + \cdots]dx.$$

Examples. — Find the differential quotient of:

1. $x^6 + x^2 - x^4$.   2. $x^7 - x^2 + x$.   3. $-x^2 + x^{10}$.

27. If a function of x is the sum of another function of x and a constant quantity, *i.e.* if

$$F(x) = f(x) + K, \qquad (1)$$

where K is a constant, then

$$F'(x) = f'(x), \qquad (2)$$

the same result as if K were not present in (1) at all. The proof of (2) is simple. When x becomes $x + \Delta x$, (1) becomes

$$F(x + \Delta x) = f(x + \Delta x) + K. \qquad (1)'$$

When we subtract (1) from (1)', K disappears entirely, and we have, after dividing by Δx,

$$\frac{F(x + \Delta x) - F(x)}{\Delta x} = \frac{f(x + \Delta x) - f(x)}{\Delta x},$$

which reduces at the limit to (2). The same result would be obtained if in (1) K were preceded by the minus instead of the plus sign.

Hence, to obtain the derivative of the sum (or difference) of a series of terms, some of which are constants, we simply take the sum (or difference) of the derivatives of all the terms which are functions of x, ignoring those which are constant.

Thus, if $y = x^3 + 5$, $\dfrac{dy}{dx} = 3x^2$.

Again, the derivative of

$$x^5 - x^4 + x + a - b - 8 \text{ is } 5x^4 - 4x^3 + 1.$$

The foregoing result is sometimes expressed by regarding all the terms, even the constants, as functions of x, and saying that the derivative of a constant term is zero.

EXAMPLES. — Find the differential quotient of:

1. $x^2 + 2$. **2.** $x^2 + 3 + x^4$. **3.** $x^3 + x^5 + 19$.

4. Prove last by general method of differentiation.

28. If a function of x is the product of a constant by another function of x, *i.e.* if

$$F(x) = K\phi(x), \tag{1}$$

then

$$F'(x) = K\phi'(x); \tag{2}$$

that is, *the derivative of the product of a constant by a function is the product of the constant by the derivative of the function.*

PROOF. — When x becomes $x + \Delta x$, (1) becomes

$$F(x + \Delta x) = K\phi(x + \Delta x). \tag{1'}$$

Subtracting (1) from (1)$'$ and dividing by Δx, we have

$$\frac{F(x + \Delta x) - F(x)}{\Delta x} = \frac{K\phi(x + \Delta x) - K\phi(x)}{\Delta x}$$

$$= K\frac{\phi(x + \Delta x) - \phi(x)}{\Delta x};$$

or at the limit, $\qquad F'(x) = K\phi'(x)$.

COROLLARY. — The derivative of mx^n is m times the derivative of x^n, as given in § 16. Hence, it is $mn\,x^{n-1}$. This result is so often used that it should be carefully memorized. When n is 1, the derivative is simply m. (Show this directly, by § 18.)

EXAMPLES. — Differentiate

$$5\,x^3,\ \ 2\,x^7,\ \ 4\,x^{10},\ \ 3\,x,\ \ \tfrac{1}{2}\,x^3,$$

$$\frac{x^6}{3},\ \ \frac{\sqrt{2}\,x^7}{5},\ \ x^8\!\left(1 + \frac{\sqrt{5}}{1 - \sqrt{2}}\right).$$

29. If a function of x is the product of two functions of x, *i.e.* if $F(x) = \phi(x)\psi(x)$, then

$$F(x + \Delta x) = \phi(x + \Delta x)\psi(x + \Delta x).$$

Subtracting and dividing by Δx, we have

$$\frac{F(x + \Delta x) - F(x)}{\Delta x} = \frac{\phi(x + \Delta x)\psi(x + \Delta x) - \phi(x)\psi(x)}{\Delta x}.$$

The right member may be changed in form without suffering any change in value by adding and subtracting $\phi(x)\psi(x + \Delta x)$ in its numerator, giving

$$\frac{\phi(x+\Delta x)\psi(x+\Delta x) - \phi(x)\psi(x) - \phi(x)\psi(x+\Delta x) + \phi(x)\psi(x+\Delta x)}{\Delta x}.$$

Grouping the terms according to common factors, we have

$$\frac{[\phi(x + \Delta x) - \phi(x)]\psi(x + \Delta x) + \phi(x)[\psi(x + \Delta x) - \psi(x)]}{\Delta x},$$

or

$$\frac{[\phi(x + \Delta x) - \phi(x)]}{\Delta x}\psi(x + \Delta x) + \frac{[\psi(x + \Delta x) - \psi(x)]}{\Delta x}\phi(x).$$

Taking these terms in order, we see that the

$$\text{limit of } \frac{\phi(x + \Delta x) - \phi(x)}{\Delta x} \text{ is } \phi'(x),$$

$$\text{limit of } \quad \psi(x + \Delta x) \quad \text{ is } \psi(x),$$

$$\text{limit of } \frac{\psi(x + \Delta x) - \psi(x)}{\Delta x} \text{ is } \psi'(x),$$

$$\text{limit of } \phi(x) \quad\quad\quad\quad \text{ is } \phi(x),$$

which gives for the limit of the right member of the equation

$$\phi'(x)\psi(x) + \psi'(x)\phi(x);$$

while for the other (or left) member of the equation the

$$\text{limit of } \frac{F(x + \Delta x) - F(x)}{\Delta x} \text{ is } F'(x).$$

Putting these limits equal, we have

$$F'(x) = \phi'(x)\psi(x) + \psi'(x)\phi(x).$$

In words, *the derivative of the product of two functions is the sum of the products obtained by multiplying the derivative of each function by the other function.*

$$\text{Thus,} \qquad \frac{d[x^2(1 + x^2)]}{dx} = \frac{d(x^2)}{dx}(1 + x^2) + \frac{d(1 + x^2)}{dx}x^2$$
$$= 2x(1 + x^2) + 2x \cdot x^2$$
$$= 2x(1 + 2x^2).$$

EXAMPLES. — **1.** Find the derivative of $(1 + x^2)(1 - x^2)$ first by § 29 and afterwards by multiplying out and then differentiating.

2. $\qquad\qquad (2 + x^3 - x^4)(5 + x^5), \quad 4(x^2 + 1)(x^3 - 2),$
$a(3x^2 + 4)(5x^3 + 6x^2 + 7x + 8), \quad (a + b)(kx^m + hx^m + p)(qx^2 + r).$

3. Prove § 28 by using § 29, regarding k as a form of $\psi(x)$, whose derivative is zero. (See § 27, end.)

4. Prove § 29, using a different notation.

30. COROLLARY. — If $F(x) = f_1(x)f_2(x)f_3(x)$, we may abbreviate $f_2(x)f_3(x)$ to $\phi(x)$, so that

$$F(x) = f_1(x)\phi(x),$$

whence $\qquad\qquad F'(x) = f_1'(x)\phi(x) + \phi'(x)f_1(x).$

Replacing $\phi(x)$ by its value $f_2(x)f_3(x)$ and $\phi'(x)$ by its value

$$f_2'(x)f_3(x) + f_3'(x)f_2(x),$$

we have

$$F'(x) = f_1'(x)\left[f_2(x)f_3(x)\right] + \left[f_2'(x)f_3(x) + f_3'(x)f_2(x)\right]f_1(x)$$
$$= f_1'(x)f_2(x)f_3(x) + f_2'(x)f_3(x)f_1(x) + f_3'(x)f_1(x)f_2(x).$$

By successive applications of § 29 this theorem can be generalized to the product of any number of functions, and in words is as follows:

The derivative of the product of any number of functions is the sum of the products obtained by multiplying the derivative of each function by the product of all the other functions.

EXAMPLES. — Find the derivatives of

$$(x^2 + 1)(x + 1)(x - 1), \quad x^3(x^2 + 2x + 3)(2x^4 - 7)(4 - x^5).$$

31. If $F(x) = \dfrac{1}{\phi(x)}$, and $\phi(x)$ is not zero, then

$$\frac{F(x + \Delta x) - F(x)}{\Delta x} = \frac{\dfrac{1}{\phi(x + \Delta x)} - \dfrac{1}{\phi(x)}}{\Delta x}$$

$$= \frac{\phi(x) - \phi(x + \Delta x)}{\Delta x \, \phi(x) \phi(x + \Delta x)}$$

$$= \frac{-1}{\phi(x) \phi(x + \Delta x)} \cdot \frac{\phi(x + \Delta x) - \phi(x)}{\Delta x},$$

or at the limit $\quad F'(x) = \dfrac{-1}{[\phi(x)]^2} \cdot \phi'(x)$

$$= \frac{-\phi'(x)}{[\phi(x)]^2}.$$

That is, the derivative of the reciprocal of a function is minus the derivative of the function divided by the square of the function.

Thus the differential quotient of $\dfrac{1}{3x^2}$ is

$$\frac{-\dfrac{d(3x^2)}{dx}}{(3x^2)^2}, \text{ or } \frac{-6x}{9x^4}, \text{ or } \frac{-2}{3x^3}.$$

32. EXAMPLES.

1. Find the derivative of

$$\frac{1}{x^4}, \quad \frac{1}{1 + x^3}, \quad \frac{1}{1 + x + x^2}. \qquad Ans. \ -\frac{4}{x^5}, \quad -\frac{3x^2}{(1 + x^3)^2}, \quad -\frac{1 + 2x}{(1 + x + x^2)^2}.$$

2. Show by method of § 29, that if

$$F(x) = \frac{\phi(x)}{\psi(x)},$$

then
$$F' = \frac{\phi'\psi - \psi'\phi}{(\psi)^2},$$

where the (x)'s are omitted for brevity.

3. Prove the same theorem by applying results of §§ 29, 31, after throwing $\dfrac{\phi}{\psi}$ in the form $\phi \cdot \dfrac{1}{\psi}$.

33. We may interject here an application of the result of § 31 to generalizing the theorem of § 16. The differential quotient of x^n was there obtained only under the restriction that n be a positive integer. But if n be a negative integer, $-m$, then x^n becomes $\dfrac{1}{x^m}$. This fraction has meaning only provided the denominator is not zero, *i.e.* x is not zero. The differential quotient becomes

$$\frac{-\,mx^{m-1}}{x^{2m}},$$

which reduces to $\qquad -\,mx^{-m-1}$ or nx^{n-1}.

That is, the restriction imposed in § 16 that n must be positive, may be removed.

Examples.

1. Differentiate x^{-2}.   **2.** Differentiate $3\,x^{-5}$.

3. Differentiate $\dfrac{1}{x^7}$.   **4.** Differentiate $\dfrac{1}{8\,x^3}$.

34. If we wish to differentiate the quotient of two functions as $\dfrac{\phi(x)}{\psi(x)}$, we can do this by combining the results of §§ 29 and 31, for the quotient may be written $\phi(x) \cdot \dfrac{1}{\psi(x)}$.

Thus, the differential quotient of $\dfrac{1 + x^2}{1 - x^3}$ is obtained by writing it $(1 + x^2)\,\dfrac{1}{1 - x^3}$. Applying the theorem for products, we get

$$(1 + x^2)\frac{d\left(\dfrac{1}{1 - x^3}\right)}{dx} + \left(\frac{1}{1 - x^3}\right)\frac{d\,(1 + x^2)}{dx},$$

'1 be reduce

If the student prefers, he may simply memorize the result of example 2, § 32, and apply.

35. If z is a function of y, and y of x, an increment Δx of x produces Δy of y, which in turn produces Δz of z.

Evidently
$$\frac{\Delta z}{\Delta x} = \frac{\Delta z}{\Delta y} \cdot \frac{\Delta y}{\Delta x}.$$

The limits of these magnitudes (assuming that definite limits exist) will therefore have the same relation, viz. :

$$\frac{dz}{dx} = \frac{dz}{dy} \cdot \frac{dy}{dx}.$$

This may also be expressed :

If
$$F(x) = \phi[f(x)],$$
then
$$F'(x) = \phi'[f(x)]f'(x).$$

It must be carefully noted that $\phi'[f(x)]$ means the derivative of $\phi[f(x)]$, *not* with respect to x, but with respect to $f(x)$. It is $\dfrac{dz}{dy}$ not $\dfrac{dz}{dx}$, or again it is $\dfrac{d\phi[f(x)]}{df(x)}$ not $\dfrac{d\phi[f(x)]}{dx}$.

In words, the derivative *with respect to x* of a function of a function of x, is the derivative of the former function *with respect to the latter*, multiplied by the derivative of the latter *with respect to x.*

Thus, if $y = (1 + x^2)^3$, $\dfrac{dy}{dx}$ may be found by denoting $(1 + x^2)$ by w, and then finding $\dfrac{dy}{dw}$ from $y = w^3$, and $\dfrac{dw}{dx}$ from $w = 1 + x^2$. Whence
$$\frac{dy}{dx} = \frac{dy}{dw} \cdot \frac{dw}{dx} = 3\,w^2 \cdot 2\,x = 3(1 + x^2)^2 2\,x.$$

But the use of w is quite unnecessary, and the student should learn to dispense with it as well as with y also. The required derivative then becomes
$$\frac{d(1 + x^2)^3}{d(1 + x^2)} \cdot \frac{d(1 + x^2)}{dx} = 3(1 + x^2)^2 2\,x.$$

Employing the notation of differentials, the process is even more easily remembered and applied. The differential of $\phi[f(x)]$ is
$$d\phi[f(x)] \text{ or } \phi'[f(x)]df(x), \text{ or } \phi'[f(x)]f'(x)dx.$$

That is, we first differentiate, treating "$f(x)$" as a single character, and our result contains $df(x)$. We then perform the further differentiation indicated by this $df(x)$.

Thus,
$$d(1 + x^2)^3 = 3(1 + x^2)^2 d(1 + x^2)$$
$$= 3(1 + x^2)^2 2\,x dx,$$

where "$(1 + x^2)$" is first kept intact as if it were not a combination of symbols, but a single cumbrous symbol.

36. EXAMPLES.

1. Differentiate $4(2 + x^3)^2$.

2. Differentiate $(7 + x)^5$.

3. Differentiate $2(1 + 2x + x^2)^3$.   *Ans.* $12(1 + x)(1 + 2x + x^2)^2$.

4. Differentiate $(3x^3 - 2)^{-4}$.

5. Differentiate $\dfrac{1}{(x^2 + x + 1)^2}$.

6. Differentiate $\dfrac{3}{(2x^3 + 3x^2 + 4)^5}$.   *Ans.* $-\dfrac{90\,x(x + 1)}{(2x^3 + 3x^2 + 4)^6}$.

7. Differentiate $a + b(1 + x^2)^2 + c(1 + x^2)^3 + k(1 + x)^5$.

8. Differentiate
$$\left(3(ax^2 + bx + c)^3 + \frac{5}{k(ax^2 + bx + c)^2}\right)(h - m(ax^2 + bx + c)^n).$$

37. In like manner, if we have a function of a function of a function, as
$$F(x) = \phi(\psi[f(x)]),$$
we may show that
$$F'(x) = \phi'[\xi(x)]\xi'(x).$$

Substituting for ξ its given value and for ξ' its value as obtained by § 35, we have
$$F'(x) = \phi'\{(\psi[f(x)])\}\psi'[f(x)]f'(x),$$

and so on for any number of functions. If we use differentials instead of differential quotients, we have
$$d\{\phi_1(\phi_2[\phi_3(\cdots)])\} = \phi_1'd\phi_2$$
$$= \phi_1'\phi_2'd\phi_3$$
$$= \phi_1'\phi_2'\phi_3'd\phi_4$$
$$= \text{etc.}$$

The proof is left to the student.

EXAMPLES.

1. Find the derivative of

$$4\{2(1 + x^2)^2 + 3(1 + x^2)^3\}^2 + 5\{2(1 + x^2)^2 + 3(1 + x^2)^3\}^3.$$

2. Differentiate $\{a + [b + (c + hx^2)^3]^5\}^2.$

38. The results of this chapter may be thus summarized:

$$\text{1.} \quad \frac{d[f_1(x) \pm f_2(x) \pm \cdots]}{dx} = f_1'(x) \pm f_2'(x) \pm \cdots.$$

$$\text{2.} \quad \frac{d[\phi(x)\psi(x)]}{dx} = \phi(x)\psi'(x) + \psi(x)\phi'(x).$$

$$\text{3.} \quad \frac{d[K\phi(x)]}{dx} = K\phi'(x).$$

$$\text{4.} \quad \frac{d\left[\dfrac{1}{\phi(x)}\right]}{dx} = \frac{-\phi'(x)}{[\phi(x)]^2}.$$

$$\text{5.} \quad \frac{d[\phi(f(x))]}{dx} = \phi'[f(x)]f'(x).$$

CHAPTER III

DIFFERENTIATION OF THE ELEMENTARY FUNCTIONS

39. We have learned (§§ 16, 33) that the derivative of x^n is nx^{n-1}, where n is any integer. x^n is the elementary algebraic function.

We have now to differentiate elementary functions called "transcendental." To do this we recur to the general method of differentiation. We first take up the trigonometric functions.

40.
$$\frac{d(\sin x)}{dx} = \lim \frac{\sin(x + \Delta x) - \sin x}{\Delta x}$$

$$= \lim \frac{\sin x \cos \Delta x + \cos x \sin \Delta x - \sin x}{\Delta x}$$

$$= \lim \left\{ \cos x \frac{\sin \Delta x}{\Delta x} - \sin x \cdot \frac{1 - \cos \Delta x}{\Delta x} \right\}$$

But $\dfrac{\sin \Delta x}{\Delta x}$ becomes unity at the limit when Δx becomes zero, and

$\dfrac{1 - \cos \Delta x}{\Delta x}$ becomes zero.

These are shown by means of Fig. 4, where AB is an arc Δx on a unit radius OA. So that BC is $\sin \Delta x$, CO is $\cos \Delta x$, and CA is $1 - \cos \Delta x$.

$$\frac{\sin \Delta x}{\Delta x} \text{ is therefore } \frac{BC}{BA},$$

and
$$\frac{1 - \cos \Delta x}{\Delta x} \text{ is } \frac{CA}{BA}.$$

When BA becomes zero, CA and BC become zero. The proof that $\lim \dfrac{BC}{BA} = 1$, and $\lim \dfrac{CA}{BA} = 0$, is left to the student with the following hints:

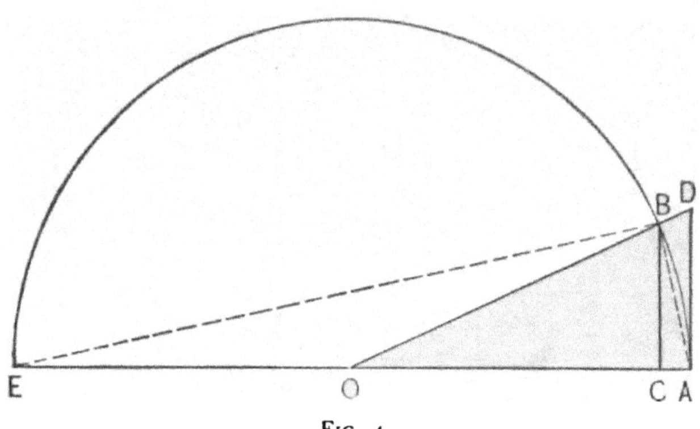

FIG. 4.

1. $1 > \dfrac{BC}{\text{arc } BA} > \dfrac{BC}{DA} = \dfrac{CO}{AO}$, which approaches 1 as limit.

2. $\dfrac{CA}{BA} = \dfrac{CA}{BC} \cdot \dfrac{BC}{BA} = \dfrac{BC}{CE} \cdot \dfrac{BC}{BA}$, which approaches 0×1.

Hence $\qquad \dfrac{d(\sin x)}{dx} = \cos x \times 1 - \sin x \times 0$

$$= \cos x.$$

In like manner, we may prove

$$\frac{d \cos x}{dx} = - \sin x.$$

41. $\qquad \dfrac{d \tan x}{dx} = \dfrac{d\left(\dfrac{\sin x}{\cos x}\right)}{dx}.$

$$= \frac{\cos x \cos x + \sin x \sin x}{\cos^2 x}$$

$$= \frac{1}{\cos^2 x}.$$

Similarly, $\qquad \dfrac{d(\cot x)}{dx} = \dfrac{-1}{\sin^2 x}.$

42.
$$\frac{d \sec x}{dx} = \frac{d\left(\dfrac{1}{\cos x}\right)}{dx} = \text{etc., according to § 31,}$$

and
$$\frac{d(\operatorname{cosec} x)}{dx} = \frac{d\left(\dfrac{1}{\sin x}\right)}{dx} = \text{etc.}$$

43.
$$\frac{d(a^x)}{dx} = \lim \frac{a^{x+\Delta x} - a^x}{\Delta x}$$
$$= \lim a^x \cdot \frac{a^{\Delta x} - 1}{\Delta x}.$$

Now let $\quad a^{\Delta x} - 1 = \delta$, so that $a^{\Delta x} = 1 + \delta$,

and $\quad\quad \Delta x \log a = \log (1 + \delta)$,

and $\quad\quad\quad \Delta x = \dfrac{\log (1 + \delta)}{\log a}$.

Then
$$\frac{d(a^x)}{dx} = \lim a^x \frac{\delta}{\dfrac{\log (1 + \delta)}{\log a}}$$
$$= \lim a^x \log a \frac{1}{\dfrac{\log (1 + \delta)}{\delta}}$$
$$= \lim a^x \log a \frac{1}{\log\{(1 + \delta)^{\frac{1}{\delta}}\}}.$$

The limit of $(1 + \delta)^{\frac{1}{\delta}}$, when δ becomes zero (which evidently occurs when Δx becomes zero) is 2.718 approximately, and is called e.*

---

* This fundamental magnitude may be pictured as follows: Suppose interest is at 4% corresponding to "25 years purchase." $\$\,1$ compounded *yearly* for this 25 years amounts to $(1.04)^{25}$. Compounded *half-yearly* for the same 25 years, it is $(1.02)^{50}$; *quarterly* $(1.01)^{100}$; *daily* $\left(1 + \frac{4}{36500}\right)^{36500/4}$; *momently*, $\lim (1 + \delta)^{\frac{1}{\delta}}$, or e. Thus e is simply the amount of $\$\,1$ at *momently* or *continuous* interest during the "purchase period." This is $\$\,2.718$, whereas with *quarterly* compounding the amount would be $\$\,2.705$, and with *yearly*, $\$\,2.666$.

Hence at the limit, $\dfrac{d(a^x)}{dx} = a^x \log a \dfrac{1}{\log e}$.

This result is independent of the system of logarithms. It is true of " common logarithms." If we take e as the base (*i.e.* employ the Naperian system), then $\log e = 1$, and the result simplifies to

$$\frac{d(a^x)}{dx} = a^x \log a.$$

Finally, if $a = e$, the result is still simpler, for $\log e = 1$. We then have

$$\frac{d(e^x)}{dx} = e^x.$$

Henceforth we shall denote common logarithms by " Log " and Naperian logarithms by " log." Any other sort of logarithms will be denoted by " $\log_b$," where the subscript b denotes the base of the system.

44. We now proceed to the inverse functions of those just considered. $y = \text{arc sin } x$, means that y is the arc whose sine is x (sometimes the notation $\sin^{-1} x$ is used), *i.e.* it means the same thing as

$$x = \sin y.$$

From this $\qquad \dfrac{dx}{dy} = \cos y$

$$= \sqrt{1 - \sin^2 y}$$

$$= \sqrt{1 - x^2}.$$

But $\dfrac{dx}{dy}$ is the reciprocal of $\dfrac{dy}{dx}$, since these expressions are the limiting values of $\dfrac{\Delta x}{\Delta y}$ and $\dfrac{\Delta y}{\Delta x}$, which are reciprocals.

Hence $\qquad \dfrac{dy}{dx} = \dfrac{1}{\sqrt{1 - x^2}}$.

Or $\qquad \dfrac{d(\text{arc sin } x)}{dx} = \dfrac{1}{\sqrt{1 - x^2}}$.

Similarly, $\qquad \dfrac{d(\text{arc cos } x)}{dx} = \dfrac{-1}{\sqrt{1 - x^2}}$.

45. If $y = \arc\tan x$, then $x = \tan y$.

$$\frac{dx}{dy} = \frac{1}{\cos^2 y}$$

$$= \sec^2 y$$

$$= 1 + \tan^2 y$$

$$= 1 + x^2.$$

Hence
$$\frac{dy}{dx} = \frac{1}{1 + x^2}.$$

Or
$$\frac{d(\arc\tan x)}{dx} = \frac{1}{1 + x^2}.$$

Similarly,
$$\frac{d(\arc\cot x)}{dx} = \frac{-1}{1 + x^2}.$$

46. If $y = \log x$, then $x = b^y$, where b is the base of the system.

Hence
$$\frac{dx}{dy} = b^y \log_b b \, \frac{1}{\log_b e}.$$

But
$$\log_b b = 1.$$

Hence
$$\frac{dx}{dy} = b^y \frac{1}{\log_b e}$$

$$= \frac{x}{\log_b e}.$$

Hence
$$\frac{dy}{dx} = \frac{\log_b e}{x}.$$

This is independent of the particular system of logarithms.

If $b = e$, then $\log_b e = 1$, and the result simplifies to

$$\frac{dy}{dx} = \frac{1}{x} \text{ or } dy = \frac{dx}{x}.$$

47. We may now still further generalize the theorem expressed in §§ 16, 33. The number n has been restricted to an integer. But if $y = x^n$ where n is *any real number*,

then
$$\log y = n \log x.$$

Taking the differential of each side,

$$\frac{dy}{y} = n \frac{dx}{x}.$$

Hence
$$\frac{dy}{dx} = \frac{ny}{x}$$
$$= \frac{nx^n}{x}$$
$$= nx^{n-1}.$$

That is, the restriction of §§ 16, 33, that n must be an integer is now removed. It may be a fraction, an irrational number, or any real number whatever.

EXAMPLES.

1. What is the differential quotient of

$$x^{\frac{3}{2}},\ x^{\frac{7}{2}},\ x^{\frac{1}{2}},\ \sqrt[3]{x},\ \sqrt[6]{x},\ x^{-\frac{1}{3}},\ \frac{1}{\sqrt{x}}?$$

2. Of $\quad \sqrt{1+x^2},\ (x^{\frac{3}{2}}-1)^{\frac{2}{3}},\ \sqrt[3]{a+b\sqrt{x}+cx^{\frac{5}{6}}}?$

48. The results of this chapter may be thus summarized :

DIRECT FUNCTIONS.

$$d(x^n) = nx^{n-1}dx.$$
$$d(mx^n) = mnx^{n-1}dx.$$
$$d(\sin x) = \cos x\,dx.$$
$$d(\cos x) = -\sin x\,dx.$$
$$d(\tan x) = \frac{dx}{\cos^2 x}.$$
$$d(\cot x) = \frac{-dx}{\sin^2 x}.$$
$$d(a^x) = \frac{a^x\,\mathrm{Log}\ a\,dx}{\mathrm{Log}\ e}$$
$$= a^x \log a\,dx.$$
$$d(e^x) = e^x dx.$$

INVERSE FUNCTIONS.

$$d(\text{arc sin } x) = \frac{dx}{\sqrt{1-x^2}}.$$
$$d(\text{arc cos } x) = \frac{-dx}{\sqrt{1-x^2}}.$$
$$d(\text{arc tan } x) = \frac{dx}{1+x^2}.$$
$$d(\text{arc cot } x) = \frac{-dx}{1+x^2}.$$
$$d(\mathrm{Log}\ x) = \frac{dx}{x}\,\mathrm{Log}\ e$$
$$d(\log x) = \frac{dx}{x}.$$

No function inverse to x^n (or to the more general form kx^n) is given, since in this case the inverse is identical in form with the direct function.

(Thus, if $y = x^n$, $x = y^{\frac{1}{n}} = y^m$, a form identical with x^n, its inverse.)

49. EXAMPLES.

1. Differentiate $3 \sin x$.

2. Differentiate $1 - a \sin x + b \cos x$.

3. Differentiate $2 \sin x \cos x$.   *Ans.* $2 \cos 2x$.

4. Differentiate $\sin x \tan x$.

5. Differentiate $\cot x + x^2 \cos x$.

6. Differentiate $\log x + \tan x \cos x$.   *Ans.* $\dfrac{1}{x} + \cos x$.

7. Differentiate $x^2 a^x$.

8. Differentiate $(a \log x - bx^2 + ca^x)(1 - x^3)$.

9. Differentiate $\sin 3x$.   *Ans.* $3 \cos 3x$.

10. Differentiate $\cos x^2$.

11. Differentiate $\tan (1 + x + x^2)$.   *Ans.* $\dfrac{1 + 2x}{\cos^2(1 + x + x^2)}$.

12. Differentiate $\log x^3 + \dfrac{1}{x} + x \tan (x + a^x - \text{arc} \cos 3x)$.

CHAPTER IV

SUCCESSIVE DIFFERENTIATION — MAXIMA AND MINIMA

50. The derivative of $2x^4$ is, as we know, $8x^3$. The derivative of $8x^3$ is, in turn, $24x^2$. The derivative of a derivative is called the *second derivative* of the original function.

When $F(x)$ stands for the original function, and $F'(x)$ for its derivative (to avoid misunderstanding we must now call it the *first* derivative), then $F''(x)$ denotes the second derivative, and $F'''(x)$ the third derivative (*i.e.* the derivative of $F''(x)$, etc.

Again, if we use the notation $\dfrac{dy}{dx}$ for the first derivative, the second derivative is evidently $\dfrac{d\left(\dfrac{dy}{dx}\right)}{dx}$, which is usually abbreviated to $\dfrac{d^2y}{dx^2}$; likewise the third or $\dfrac{d\left(\dfrac{d^2y}{dx^2}\right)}{dx}$ is written $\dfrac{d^3y}{dx^3}$, and so on to $\dfrac{d^4y}{dx^4}, \dfrac{d^5y}{dx^5}$, etc.

51. EXAMPLES.

1. What is the third derivative of x^5?

2. What are the 2d, 3d, 4th derivatives of x^2?

3. Differentiate successively ax^n. When, if ever, will the answers become zero? What sort of a number must n be to bring about such a result?

4. Differentiate successively $\sin x$. *Ans.* $\cos x$, $-\sin x$, $-\cos x$, $\sin x$

5. Differentiate successively $\tan x$.

6. Differentiate successively a^x.

7. Differentiate successively $\arcsin x$.

8. Differentiate successively $\arctan x$.

$$Ans. \quad \frac{1}{1+x^2}, \quad -\frac{2x}{(1+x^2)^2}, \quad -\frac{2(1-3x^2)}{(1+x^2)^3}.$$

9. Differentiate successively $\log x$.

52. Just as the first derivative threw light on the problems of velocity, tangential slope, etc., so the second derivative will illuminate *acceleration, curvature,* etc.

We have seen that if for a falling body $s = 16\,t^2$, then

$$\frac{ds}{dt} = 32\,t, \tag{1}$$

whence

$$\frac{d^2s}{dt^2} = 32. \tag{2}$$

We may understand this result better if we designate $\frac{ds}{dt}$ by v, as in § 6, so that (1) becomes

$$v = 32\,t, \tag{1'}$$

and (2)

$$\frac{dv}{dt} = 32, \tag{2'}$$

where $\frac{dv}{dt}$ is evidently simply

$$\frac{d^2s}{dt^2},$$

for both are mere abbreviations of

$$\frac{d\left(\frac{ds}{dt}\right)}{dt}.$$

What does equation (2) or (2)' mean? $\frac{dv}{dt}$ *means the rate at which the body is gaining speed.* It is clear that moving bodies do gain or lose speed, and that some gain or lose faster than others.

The gain or loss of speed has nothing to do with how fast a body is going. A slowly moving body may be *gaining* speed very fast, while a fast moving body may not be gaining at all, or may even be losing speed.

If we use the term *velo* to indicate a unit of velocity, or one foot per second, we know from (1) that a body which has fallen 2 seconds has then a speed of 64 velos, while at the end of 5 seconds its speed is 160 velos. Here is a gain of 96 velos in 3 seconds, or an average of 32 velos per second.

This does not, of course, imply that the body had gained at the rate of 32 velos per second all the time. But equation (2) tells us that this is the case. A falling body on the earth is *constantly* gaining velocity at the rate of 32 velos per second.

Rate of *gain of velocity* is called acceleration, and we see, therefore, that a falling body is a case of " uniformly accelerated motion."

Observe that the acceleration or rate of gain of velocity expressed in 32 velos per second, cannot be expressed as any number of *feet per second.* On the contrary, substituting for the word " velos " its definition " feet-per-second," we see that 32 velos per second is 32 *feet per second per second.*

If the distance a body moves in time t is not $16\,t^2$, but $10\,t^3$, then its velocity is $30\,t^2$, and acceleration $60\,t$. In other words, its acceleration in this case depends on the time. If the body has fallen 2 seconds, its acceleration is 120 velos per second ; if 3, 180 velos per second ; etc.

53. If $F(x)$ expresses the ordinate of any point on a curve when the abscissa is x, we have seen that $F'(x)$ expresses the tangential slope at that point. What does $F''(x)$ represent? Evidently the rate at which that slope is changing at that particular point as x increases. It denotes what we may call the *curvature* at that point with respect to the axis of x.

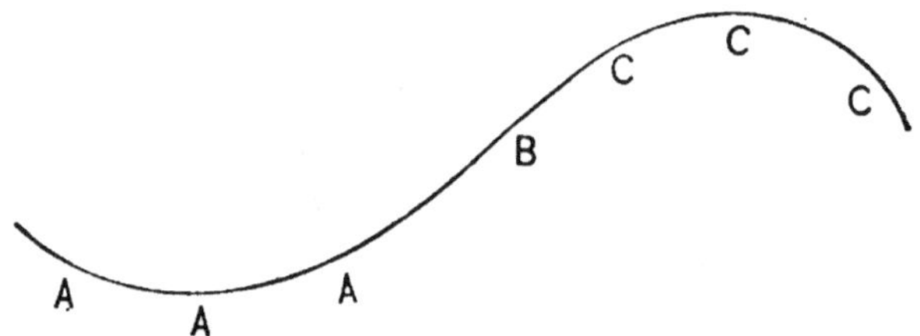

FIG. 5. — A, rate of gain of slope positive ; B ("point of inflection"), zero ; C, negative.

Curvature, however, is usually measured with respect to the tangent itself. The expression for this, the more proper sense of curvature, is somewhat more complicated. At a point when the curve is horizontal, the two sorts of curvature are identical.

54. When the curve is horizontal, the slope of the tangent $F'(x)$ is, as has been seen, zero. But the curve may be horizontal at three sorts of points : a maximum as at A

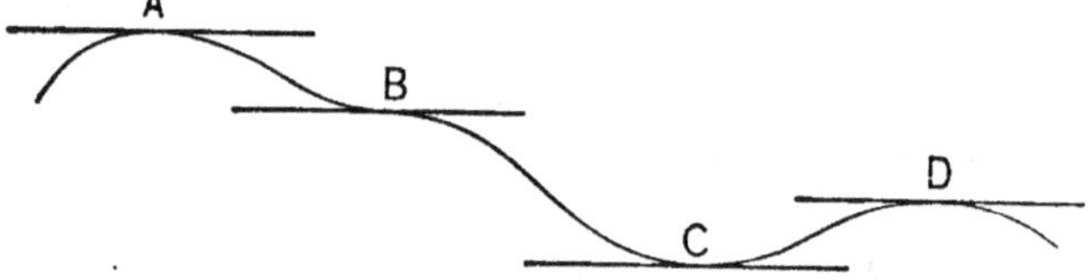

FIG. 6. — Points of zero slope: A, maximum: B, horizontal point of inflection; C, minimum; D, maximum.

and D (Fig. 6), or a minimum as at C, or a horizontal point of inflection as at B.

A maximum point on a curve is a point such that the ordinate, or y, of that point is larger than the ordinates of points in its neighborhood on either side. (The phrase

" points in its neighborhood " means all points on the curve within some small but finite distance on either side.) A minimum point is one whose ordinate is less than the ordinates in its neighborhood on either side. A point of inflection is one where the neighboring parts of the curve on opposite sides of the point are also on opposite sides of the tangent as at B in Figs. 5 and 6.

In the neighborhood at the left of a maximum the slope of the curve is positive, while on the right it is negative. For a minimum, the slope is negative on the left and positive on the right. For a horizontal point of inflection, the slope is positive on both sides or else negative on both sides.

It is to be observed that a curve may have more than one maximum or minimum, and that a maximum ordinate does *not* mean the greatest ordinate of all, but only the greatest *in its neighborhood.* Thus the ordinate at D is a maximum, though that at A is larger.

55. Dropping the symbolism of the curve, it is clear that when a function $F(x)$ reaches a maximum or minimum, then $F'(x) = 0$, for $F'(x)$ represents the rate of increase of $F(x)$, and at a maximum or minimum this rate is zero.

But if, conversely, we have $F'(x) = 0$, we simply know that for that particular value of x which satisfies this equation $F(x)$ is not increasing nor decreasing. We cannot tell whether it is a maximum or a minimum or an " inflectional stationary " value (*i.e.* one such that $F(x)$ will increase for a change of x in one direction and decrease for a change of x in the other direction).

56. Now these questions can be settled by recourse to the second derivative, provided this is not also zero.

If the second derivative be positive, the function is a minimum ; if it be negative, it is a maximum. This will be clear if we remind ourselves of the meaning of the second derivative. It indicates the rate of change of the slope. If positive, it means the slope is increasing ; if negative, it means the slope is decreasing.

If, therefore, at a point where the first derivative or slope is zero, the second derivative or "curvature" (§ 53) is positive, we know that at that point the slope is *increasing*. But as its present value is zero, it must be changing from a *negative* to a *positive* value. This can evidently only occur at a minimum. *Per contra*, if the second derivative is negative, it indicates a slope growing *less*, *i.e.* (as the slope is now zero) changing from positive to negative. This evidently occurs at the maximum, and nowhere else.

Thus, take the function $x^3 - 27x$. This has for first derivative $3x^2 - 27$, and for second derivative $6x$. Putting the first expression equal to zero and solving, we find $x = \pm 3$; that is, the function $x^3 - 27x$ has two points at which it is stationary (or the tangent is horizontal), where x is 3, and where x is -3. The first of these is a minimum, and the second a maximum ; for the second derivative $6x$ is positive for $x = 3$, and negative for $x = -3$.

57. The exceptional case mentioned in § 56 (viz. where the value of x, which renders the first derivative zero, also renders the second derivative zero) seldom occurs in practice. When it does occur, we cannot decide the nature of the function for that point, without recourse to the third derivative. If this be positive, the function is neither at a maximum nor minimum, but at a horizontal point of inflection, as at A (Fig. 7), when, for an increase of x, the function was increasing, both before and after the point. If, on the other hand, it be negative, the function is at a horizontal point of inflection as at B

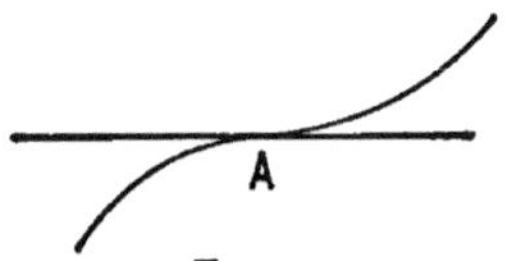

Fig. 7.

(Fig. 6), when the function was decreasing both before and after reaching this point. If, finally, it be zero, we are again left in the dark as to the nature of the function, and must proceed to the fourth derivative. We employ this just as if it were the second. If it turns out zero, and forces us to consider the fifth, we employ this just as if it were the third, and so on.

That is, *as long as the successive derivatives turn out zero, we go on until we find one which is not zero. If this derivative be of an* EVEN *order (i.e.* 2d, 4th, 6th, etc., derivative), *we know that the function is either a maximum or a minimum, and is the one or the other according as the derivative in question is negative or positive.* But if the derivative which does not vanish is of an *odd* order (*i.e.* 3d, 5th, etc.), we know that the function is neither at a maximum or minimum value, but at a point of horizontal inflection and is increasing or decreasing according as the derivative is positive or negative.

58. We shall not devote the requisite space here to proving the truth of the last section in full, but shall merely indicate the first step, leaving the student, if he so desires, to extend the demonstration.

Suppose in testing the function $F(x)$ we find for the value of x which renders $F'(x) = 0$, that $F''(x)$ is also zero, but $F'''(x)$ is positive. Denoting this value of x by x_1, we may state the problem as follows : given

$$F'(x_1) = 0,$$
$$F''(x_1) = 0,$$
$$F'''(x_1) > 0,$$

to discover the nature of $F(x_1)$.

We shall solve this by reasoning from F''' successively back to F'', F', and F.

Since $F'''(x_1)$ is positive, it shows that $F''(x)$ is *increasing* as x increases. But as $F''(x_1)$ is zero, the fact that $F''(x)$ is increasing shows that it was negative before reaching $F''(x_1)$ and positive after. This is our conclusion for F''.

Since $F''(x)$ was, negative before reaching $F''(x_1)$ it shows that $F'(x)$ was *then* decreasing, and since $F''(x)$ was positive afterward, $F'(x)$ was *then* increasing.

But, if $F'(x)$ is zero at $F'(x_1)$ and was decreasing before and increasing after, it must have been positive both before and after. This is our conclusion for F'. Since F' is positive both before and after, it shows that $F(x)$ was increasing both before and after, and is therefore not a maximum, but a horizontal point of inflection.

Thus let $F(x)$ be

$$x^4 - 6x^2 + 8x + 7.$$

Then $\qquad\qquad\qquad F'$ is $4x^3 - 12x + 8.$

Then $\qquad\qquad\qquad\quad F''$ is $12x^2 - 12.$

Then $\qquad\qquad\qquad\qquad F'''$ is $24x.$

The roots of $F' = 0$ are 1 and -2. For $x = 1$, F'' vanishes, but F''' is positive. Hence we know that F or $x^4 - 6x^2 + 8x + 7$ is at a stationary inflectional value increasing on either side, as x increases.

But for $x = -2$, F'' is positive. Hence for this value of x, F is a minimum.

59. EXAMPLES. —**1.** Find maximum or minimum value of x^2.

2. Find maximum or minimum value of $3x^2 - 27x$.

3. Find maximum or minimum value of $2x^2 + x + 1$.

4. Find maximum or minimum value of $x^3 - 12x + 6$.

5. Find maximum or minimum value of $2x^3 + 6x^2 + 6x + 5$.

6. Find maximum or minimum value of $x^3 - 2x + 3x^2 - 4$.

7. What is the nature of $x^4 - 24x^2 + 64x + 10$ for $x = 2$?

8. What is the nature of $x^4 + 4x^3 + 6x^2 + 4x + 17$ for $x = -1$?

60. If $F(x)$ is of the form $\phi(x) + K$, where K is any constant, then the same values of x render $F(x)$ a maximum or minimum as render $\phi(x)$ a maximum or minimum respectively.

For the nature of $F(x)$ or of $\phi(x)$ as to maxima and minima depends exclusively on the nature of their derivatives, and the derivatives of these two functions (viz., $\phi(x) + K$ and $\phi(x)$) are evidently identical.

Thus to find the value of x to render

$$x^2 + 2\left(1 + \frac{1}{\sqrt{2}}\right)$$

a maximum or minimum, we may drop the constant term and simply inquire for what value of x the form x^2 is a maximum or minimum.

61. If $F(x)$ is of the form $K\phi(x)$ when K is a *positive* constant, then the values of x which render $F(x)$ a maximum or minimum are the same as those which render $\phi(x)$ a maximum or minimum respectively.

If $F(x) = K\phi(x)$ where K is a *negative* constant, then the values of x which render $F(x)$ a maximum or minimum are the same as those which render $\phi(x)$ a minimum or maximum respectively.

For the successive derivatives of these two functions (viz., $K\phi(x)$ and $\phi(x)$) are

$$\left.\begin{array}{c} K\phi'(x) \\ K\phi''(x) \\ \text{etc.} \end{array}\right\} \text{ and } \left\{\begin{array}{l} \phi'(x), \\ \phi''(x), \\ \text{etc.,} \end{array}\right.$$

and evidently the very same values of x will make the two first derivatives zero, and, if K be positive, will make the two second derivatives of the same sign or both zero; but if K be negative, will make them of the opposite sign or both zero. Similarly for the two third derivatives, etc. Since the natures of F and of ϕ, as respects maxima and minima, depend exclusively on the signs $(+, -,$ or $0)$ of their derivatives, the theorem is proved.

Thus, to obtain the value of x which will make

$$\left(1 - \frac{1}{\sqrt{2}}\right)(x^2 - x)$$

a maximum or minimum, we drop the constant factor (which is evidently positive) and find out which values of x make $x^2 - x$, a maximum or minimum.

EXAMPLES. — **1.** Interpret the theorems of §§ 60, 61 geometrically.

2. Find maximum or minimum of $5(1 + x + x^2) + 10$.

3. Find maximum or minimum of $-3x\left(x + 1 + \dfrac{17}{x}\right)$.

4. Find maximum or minimum of $m\left\{\dfrac{a(x^2 + bx + c) + e}{h} + k\right\}$.

62. The subject of maxima and minima is one of the most important in the Calculus, and has innumerable applications in Geometry, Physics, and Economics.

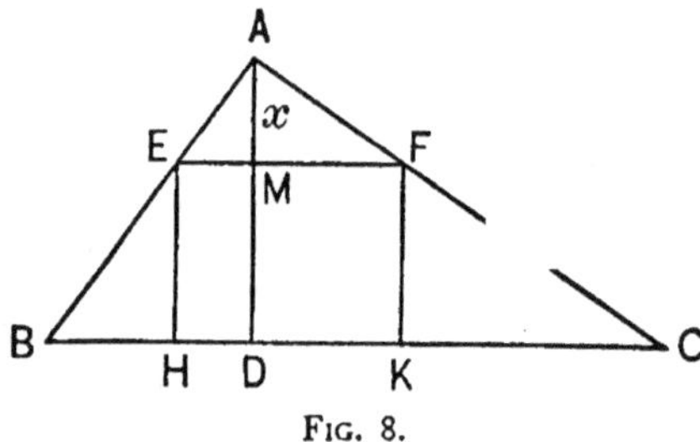

FIG. 8.

Let ABC (Fig. 8) be any triangle, and $EFKH$ a rectangle inscribed within it. This inscribed rectangle will vary in size according to its position. If too low and flat, it is small. If too high and thin, it is also small. Between these positions there must be a position of maximum, where the area is the largest possible.

Now its area is the product of the base HK or EF by the altitude DM, and the problem consists in discovering where $EF \cdot DM$ is a maximum.

To do this, we must first express EF and DM in terms of some one variable. Out of the many possible (*e.g.* BH, BK, AE, FC, EH, HK, etc.) we select AM, and denote it by x. We call $AD = h$ and $BC = a$. Evidently $MD = h - x$. To express EF in terms of x, we proceed as follows : The triangles AEF and ABC are similar, so that their bases and altitudes are proportional. That is,

$$\frac{AM}{AD} = \frac{EF}{BC} \quad \text{or} \quad \frac{x}{h} = \frac{EF}{a},$$

whence
$$EF = \frac{ax}{h}.$$

Consequently
$$EF \times DM = (h - x)\frac{ax}{h}.$$

We wish to know for what value of x this expression is a maximum. We may omit the positive constant factor $\frac{a}{h}$, leaving

$$(h - x)x \text{ or } hx - x^2,$$

the first differential of which is $h - 2x$,

which, put equal to zero and solved, gives

$$x = \frac{h}{2},$$

the required answer.

We are sure it is a maximum and not a minimum or stationary inflectional value, since the second differential is -2; *i.e.* negative.

We have learned, therefore, that the maximum rectangle inscribed in a triangle is that whose altitude is half the altitude of the triangle.

In physics many important principles depend upon maxima and minima. Thus the equilibrium of a pool of water, a pendulum, a rocking chair, or a suspension bridge, is determined by the condition that the centre of gravity in each case shall be at the lowest possible point.

In economics we have the principle of maximum consumer's rent, of maximum profit under a monopoly, etc.

63. EXAMPLES.

1. How must a given straight line be divided so that the product of its two parts shall be a maximum ?

2. What is the minimum amount of tin necessary to make a cylindrical vessel which will have a given capacity A? What must be the relation between the height h and the radius of the base r?

3. Find the maximum cylinder inscribed in a circular cone of revolution. *Ans.* Altitude of cylinder equals one third that of the cone.

4. Find the maximum rectangle inscribed in a semicircle.

Ans. The sides are $\frac{r}{2}\sqrt{2}$, and $r\sqrt{2}$.

5. A cylinder of revolution has a given diameter. What altitude must it have in order that it may have the least total area in proportion to its volume?

HINT. — Express volume and total area in terms of the variable altitude x, and the constant radius r. Then find when

$$\frac{\text{total area}}{\text{volume}} \text{ is a minimum.}$$

6. If the function $pF(p)$ is continuous, what equation gives a value of p which makes the function a maximum?

Write the algebraic expression denoting the condition under which the value of p, in the equation asked for, corresponds to a maximum or minimum.

7. If the price, p, of an article is fixed and the cost of producing it, for a given individual, is a function $F(x)$, of the quantity produced, x, how much must he produce to make his profit, $xp - F(x)$, a maximum or minimum? Express this result in words. What condition must $F(x)$ satisfy that the profit may be a maximum and not a minimum? Express this condition in words.

8. Four equal squares with side x are removed from the corners of a square piece of cardboard with side c and the sides are turned up so as to form an open square box. If the square box is to be of maximum volume, what will be the value of x in terms of c? *Ans.* $\frac{c}{6}$.

9. The distance between two points, B and C, on a coast is 5 miles. A person in a boat is 3 miles distant from B, his nearest shore point. Supposing he can walk 5 miles an hour and can row 4 miles an hour, what distance from C should he land in order to reach C in the shortest possible time? *Ans.* 1 mile.

10. Given l, the slant height of a right cone; find the altitude when the volume is a maximum. *Ans.* $\frac{l}{3}\sqrt{3}$.

CHAPTER V

TAYLOR'S THEOREM

64. We know that certain functions can be developed in terms of powers of variables. Thus $(a + x)^4$ becomes by the binomial theorem

$$a^4 + 4\,a^3x + 6\,a^2x^2 + 4\,ax^3 + x^4.$$

Again, by simple division, we may show that (provided x lies between -1 and $+1$)

$$\frac{1}{1+x} = 1 - x + x^2 - x^3 + \cdots.$$

Now the Calculus supplies a much simpler and more general method than algebra of developing functions in series of this sort.

Thus, let $\phi(x)$ be any function of x *developable in the form*

$$\phi(x) = A + B(x - a) + C(x - a)^2 + D(x - a)^3 + \cdots,$$

where a, A, B, C, etc., are constants, and the series converges. We shall show how to express the "undetermined coefficients" A, B, C, etc., in terms of the single constant a.

By successive differentiation, we have *

$$\phi'(x) = B + 2\,C(x - a) + 3\,D(x - a)^2 + \cdots$$
$$\phi''(x) = \quad + 2\,C \quad\quad\quad + 2\cdot 3\,D(x - a) + \cdots$$

etc.

* By § 26 which can readily be extended so as to apply to an infinite number of terms if, as is here assumed, the sum of these terms converges.

Since these equations (and the original from which they are derived) are true for any value of x, they are true when $x = a$.

They then become

$$\phi(a) = A, \qquad \text{or} \quad A = \phi(a);$$
$$\phi'(a) = 1 \cdot B, \qquad B = \phi'(a);$$
$$\phi''(a) = 1 \cdot 2\, C, \qquad C = \frac{\phi''(a)}{2!};$$
$$\phi'''(a) = 1 \cdot 2 \cdot 3\, D, \qquad D = \frac{\phi'''(a)}{3!};$$

etc.,

where $2!$ means $1 \cdot 2$ and $3!$ means $1 \cdot 2 \cdot 3$, etc.

Substituting these values of A, B, C, D, etc., we have

$$\phi(x) = \phi(a) + \phi'(a)(x-a) + \phi''(a)\frac{(x-a)^2}{2!}$$
$$+ \phi'''(a)\frac{(x-a)^3}{3!} + \cdots.$$

65. This series, which is "Taylor's theorem," expresses the magnitude of the function ϕ for any value of x in terms of its magnitude and that of its derivatives for any *other* value of x.

Thus if we could write down some exact formula $y = \phi(x)$ for the population (y) of the United States in reference to the time (x) elapsed since, say 1800, Taylor's Theorem tells us that we could get the population in 1900, $\phi(x)$, merely from data of the census of 1890.

As a first approximation we take the population of 1890 itself, $\phi(a)$. But, as the population has not remained stationary, we add a correction for the increase within the decade.

This increase we first assume to be $(x-a)\,\phi'(a)$, *i.e.* the rate of increase known to exist in 1890, $\phi'(a)$, multiplied by the time between the two censuses $(x-a)$. But since the rate of increase (by which is here meant so many thousand souls per year, not the *percentage* rate) has not remained stationary, we add another correction $\dfrac{\phi''(a)(x-a)^2}{1 \cdot 2}$, constructed on the supposition that the rate of increase *of* the rate of increase of population, $\phi''(a)$, known to exist in 1890 has remained constant until 1900. Not content with this, we take into account the rate of increase of the rate of increase of the rate of increase of population, and so on.

66. Geometrically, the theorem states that the ordinate of any point of the curve $y = \phi(x)$ can be obtained from the ordinate, slope, "curvature," etc., of any other point.

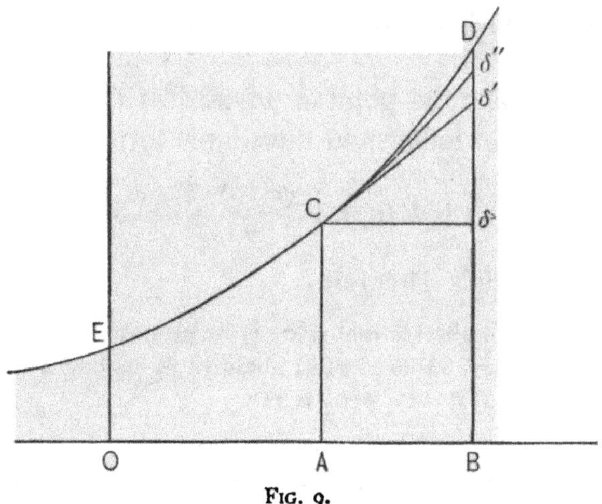

FIG. 9.

Thus, OB (Fig. 9) is x and BD, $\phi(x)$; OA is a and AC, $\phi(a)$. The theorem tells us that the ordinate of the point D can be ascertained purely from the data as to the curve at C, viz. its height, the rate at which this height is increasing (*i.e.* its slope), the rate at which this slope is increasing (*i.e.* its "curvature" (§ 53)), the rate at which this "curvature" is increasing, etc., etc. In fact, the theorem states that the ordinate DB is the sum of various magnitudes: first, $\phi(a)$, which is represented by $B\delta$ (for this is the same as AC); secondly, $(x-a)\phi'(a)$, which is represented by $\delta\delta'$ (for $\dfrac{\delta\delta'}{C\delta}$ is the slope of the curve at C, and so $= \phi'(a)$, hence $\delta\delta' = C\delta \times \phi'(a) = (x-a)\phi'(a))$, thirdly, $\dfrac{(x-a)^2\phi''(a)}{2!}$, which is represented by $\delta'\delta''$, when δ'' is reached by drawing the curve $C\delta''$, which has the same curvature as the principal curve CD has at the point C, but retains that "curvature" (with respect to the x-axis, see § 53) throughout; that is, we approach D by adding successive corrections. δ is the position D would have had if the ordinate of the curve had remained unchanged from C (so that the curve would have followed the horizontal $C\delta$); δ' is the position D would have had if the rate of increase of the ordinate, *i.e.* the slope of the curve, had remained unchanged from C (so that the curve would have followed $C\delta'$); δ'' is the position D would have taken if the rate of increase of the slope had remained unchanged from C (so that the curve would have followed $C\delta''$), etc.

67. If we take the point E instead of C, so that $a = 0$, Taylor's theorem reduces to the simple form

$$\phi(x) = \phi(0) + \phi'(0)x + \frac{\phi''(0)x^2}{2!} + \frac{\phi'''(0)x^3}{3!} + \text{etc.}$$

This is Maclaurin's Theorem.

The student will observe that $\phi(0)$ is by no means itself zero. It is simply that particular value of $\phi(x)$ obtained by putting $x = 0$. Thus, if $\phi(x)$ is $x^3 + 2x^2 + 117$, $\phi(0)$ is 117.

68. A second mode of stating Taylor's Theorem, and one often met with, is obtained by denoting the difference of abscissas $x - a$ by h, and replacing x by $a + h$ (for, if $x - a = h$, $x = a + h$), so that

$$\phi(a+h) = \phi(a) + \phi'(a)h + \phi''(a)\frac{h^2}{2!} + \frac{\phi'''(a)h^3}{3!} + \cdots,$$

or, changing our notation from a to x,

$$\phi(x+h) = \phi(x) + \phi'(x)h + \phi''(x)\frac{h^2}{2!} + \cdots,$$

where x now refers to the abscissa of C instead of that of D.

The student will also sometimes see the theorem expressed in the same form, but with y employed in place of h.

69. There are many applications of Taylor's theorem in economics. Cournot in his *Principes Mathématiques* makes frequent use of it, as does Pareto in his *Cours d'économie politique.*

When h is a small quantity, as in some of Cournot's cases of taxation, then the higher powers of h may be neglected, and we have the approximate formula

$$\phi(x + h) = \phi(x) + h\phi'(x).$$

This is assuming that if the interval AB is very small, the point δ' will coincide approximately with D.

70. It will be observed that an hiatus was indicated in the demonstration of Taylor's Theorem. This means that it is not always possible to develop $\phi(x)$ in the series proposed, and that the attempt to do so will give a diverging or indeterminate series.

It is impossible in so elementary a treatise as this to indicate in what cases Taylor's Theorem is applicable. The subject is one of great difficulty, and some of the most important conclusions relating to it have only recently been discovered.

71. To show the application of Taylor's and Maclaurin's theorems, let us use them to develop the function $(a + x)^n$, assuming it developable. Since $\phi(x) = (a + x)^n$,

$$\phi'(x) = n(a + x)^{n-1},$$

$$\phi''(x) = n(n - 1)(a + x)^{n-2},$$

etc.

Hence

$$\phi(\mathrm{o}) = a^n,$$
$$\phi'(\mathrm{o}) = na^{n-1},$$
$$\phi''(\mathrm{o}) = n(n-\mathrm{I})a^{n-2}, \ .$$

etc.

Hence

$$\phi(x) = \phi(\mathrm{o}) + \phi'(\mathrm{o})x + \frac{\phi''(\mathrm{o})x^2}{2\,!} + \cdots$$

$$= a^n + na^{n-1}x + \frac{n(n-\mathrm{I})a^{n-2}x^2}{2\,!} + \cdots,$$

a result which we already know by the binomial theorem.

Again let us develop $\sin x$, assuming it developable.

Since

$$\phi(x) = \sin x \qquad\qquad \phi(\mathrm{o}) = \mathrm{o},$$
$$\phi'(x) = \cos x \qquad\qquad \phi'(\mathrm{o}) = \mathrm{I},$$
$$\phi''(x) = -\sin x \qquad\qquad \phi''(\mathrm{o}) = \mathrm{o},$$
$$\phi'''(x) = -\cos x \qquad\qquad \phi'''(\mathrm{o}) = -\mathrm{I}.$$

etc.   etc.

Hence

$$\phi(x) = \phi(\mathrm{o}) + \phi'(\mathrm{o})x + \frac{\phi''(\mathrm{o})x^2}{2\,!} + \frac{\phi'''(\mathrm{o})x^3}{3\,!} + \cdots$$

$$= \mathrm{o} + x + \mathrm{o} - \frac{x^3}{3\,!} + \cdots$$

$$= x - \frac{x^3}{3\,!} + \frac{x^5}{5\,!} - \frac{x^7}{7\,!} + \cdots.$$

Again let us take
$$\frac{\mathrm{I}}{x - a + \mathrm{I}}.$$

Since $\phi(x) = \dfrac{\mathrm{I}}{x - a + \mathrm{I}},$ $\phi(a) = \mathrm{I},$

$$\phi'(x) = -(x - a + \mathrm{I})^{-2}, \qquad\qquad \phi'(a) = -\mathrm{I},$$
$$\phi''(x) = 2(x - a + \mathrm{I})^{-3}, \qquad\qquad \phi''(a) = 2,$$
$$\phi'''(x) = -2\cdot 3(x - a + \mathrm{I})^{-4}, \qquad \phi'''(a) = -3\,!.$$

Hence, by Taylor's Theorem,

$$\phi(x) = \mathrm{I} - (x - a) + \frac{2(x - a)^2}{2\,!} - \frac{3\,!(x - a)^3}{3\,!} + \cdots.$$

72. Among other important uses of Taylor's and Maclaurin's theorems are the evaluations of the fundamental constants e and π.

To obtain e, we develop the function e^x.

$$\phi(x) = e^x, \qquad\qquad \phi(0) = 1,$$
$$\phi'(x) = e^x, \qquad\qquad \phi'(0) = 1,$$
$$\phi''(x) = e^x, \qquad\qquad \phi''(0) = 1,$$
$$\text{etc.} \qquad\qquad\qquad \text{etc.}$$

Since $\quad \phi(x) = \phi(0) + \phi'(0)x + \dfrac{\phi''(0)x^2}{2} + \dfrac{\phi'''(0)x^3}{3!} + \cdots,$

we have $\qquad\qquad e^x = 1 + x + \dfrac{x^2}{2} + \dfrac{x^3}{3!} + \cdots.$

If, in this equation, we put $x = 1$, we have

$$e = 1 + 1 + \frac{1}{2} + \frac{1}{3!} + \frac{1}{4!} + \cdots,$$

from which e may be computed with any required degree of approximation. $e = 2.71828 \cdots$.

To obtain π, develop arc tan x.

$$\phi(x) = \text{arc tan } x, \qquad\qquad \phi(0) = 0,$$
$$\phi'(x) = \frac{1}{1 + x^2}, \qquad\qquad \phi'(0) = 1.$$

If x be less than unity, we know by algebra that *

$$\phi'(x) = \frac{1}{1 + x^2} = 1 - x^2 + x^4 - x^6 + \cdots.$$

Hence $\quad \phi''(x) = -2x + 4x^3 - 6x^5 + \cdots, \qquad \phi''(0) = 0,$

$\qquad \phi'''(x) = -2 + 3\cdot4x^2 - 5\cdot6x^4 + \cdots, \quad \phi'''(0) = -2,$

$\qquad \phi^{iv}(x) = 2\cdot3\cdot4x - 4\cdot5\cdot6x^3 + \cdots, \qquad \phi^{iv}(0) = 0,$

$\qquad \phi^{v}(x) = 2\cdot3\cdot4 - 3\cdot4\cdot5\cdot6x^2 + \cdots, \qquad \phi^{v}(0) = +4!,$

$$\text{etc.} \qquad\qquad\qquad\qquad \text{etc.}$$

$$\phi(x) = \phi(0) + \phi'(0)x + \frac{\phi''(0)x^2}{2} + \frac{\phi'''(0)x^3}{3!} + \cdots$$

$$\text{arc tan } x = 0 + x + 0 + \frac{-2x^3}{3!} + 0 + \frac{4!\,x^5}{5!} + \cdots$$

$$= x - \frac{x^3}{3} + \frac{x^5}{5} - \frac{x^7}{7} + \cdots.$$

* It is assumed here, without proof, that the proper conditions as to convergence are fulfilled.

Let x be $\dfrac{1}{\sqrt{3}}$, so that arc tan x, the arc whose tangent is $\dfrac{1}{\sqrt{3}}$, is $\dfrac{\pi}{6}$.
(*i.e.* an arc of thirty degrees). The preceding equation then becomes:

$$\frac{\pi}{6} = \frac{1}{\sqrt{3}} - \frac{1}{3(\sqrt{3})^3} + \frac{1}{5(\sqrt{3})^5} - \cdots$$

$$= \frac{1}{\sqrt{3}}\left[1 - \frac{1}{3\cdot 3} + \frac{1}{5\cdot 3^2} - \frac{1}{7\cdot 3^3} + \cdots \right],$$

whence $\qquad \pi = 2\sqrt{3}\left[1 - \frac{1}{3\cdot 3} + \frac{1}{5\cdot 3^2} - \frac{1}{7\cdot 3^3} + \cdots \right]$

$$= 3.14159\cdots.$$

73. EXAMPLES.

1. Develop $(a - x)^{-2}$ in series of ascending powers of x.

2. Develop $\sqrt{a - x}$.

3. Develop $\cos x$. *Ans.* $1 - \dfrac{x^2}{2!} + \dfrac{x^4}{4!} - \dfrac{x^6}{6!} + \cdots$.

4. Develop $\log (1 + x)$.

5. Develop a^{b+x}.

6. Develop e^{3x}. *Ans.* $1 + 3x + \dfrac{9x^2}{2!} + \dfrac{27x^3}{3!}$.

7. Develop $\frac{1}{2}(e^x - e^{-x})$.

8. Develop arc sin x. *Ans.* $x + \dfrac{1}{2}\cdot\dfrac{x^3}{3} + \dfrac{1\cdot 3}{2\cdot 4}\cdot\dfrac{x^5}{5} + \dfrac{1\cdot 3\cdot 5}{2\cdot 4\cdot 6}\cdot\dfrac{x^7}{7} + \cdots$.

9. Develop $\cos^2 x$.

10. Develop $e^x \sec x$.

11. Develop $\log (1 + \sin x)$. *Ans.* $x - \dfrac{x^2}{2} + \dfrac{x^3}{6} - \dfrac{x^4}{12} + \cdots$.

12. Develop arc tan x.

13. Develop $\cos (x + y)$.

$\qquad$ *Ans.* $\cos x - y \sin x - \dfrac{y^2}{2!}\cos x + \dfrac{y^3}{3!}\sin x + \cdots$.

14. Develop $\tan (x + y)$.

Ans. $\tan x + y \sec^2 x + y^2 \sec^2 x \tan x + \dfrac{y^3}{3}\sec^2 x(1 + 3\tan^2 x) + \cdots$.

CHAPTER VI

INTEGRAL CALCULUS

74. We have thus far been occupied with the derivation from F of F', F'', etc. But it is possible to reverse this process, and, given F''', or any other derivative, to pass back to F'', F', F.

$F'(x)$ was called the *derivative* of $F(x)$; we now name $F(x)$ the *primitive* of $F'(x)$. The first process of obtaining F' from F is the subject matter of the *differential calculus*, of which the preceding chapters have treated. The process of obtaining F from F' is the subject matter of the *integral calculus*.

75. In the differential calculus, we saw that the result of differentiation was expressed either in the differential quotient $F'(x)$, or in the differential $F'(x)dx$. In the integral calculus it is customary to employ only the latter form. We called $F'(x)dx$ the *differential* of $F(x)$; we now call $F(x)$ the *integral* of $F'(x)dx$. We obtained $F'(x)dx$ from $F(x)$ by *differentiation*. We obtain $F(x)$ from $F'(x)dx$ by *integration*. The symbol of differentiation was d; that of integration is $\int$.

Knowing that $d(x^2) = 2\,x\,dx$, we may write $\int 2\,x\,dx = x^2$; or again, since

$$dF(x) = F'(x)dx$$

expresses in the most general manner the process of the differential calculus,

$$\int F'(x)dx = F(x)$$

expresses the process of the integral calculus. Both equations state the same fact looked at from opposite directions. The former equation reads, " the differential of $F(x)$ is $F'(x)dx$"; the latter may be read, " the function-of-which-the-differential-is $F'(x)dx$ is $F(x)$," for the hyphened words are what is meant by " integral of."

The simplest form of the above equation is $\int dx = x$.

76. The symbol $\int$ was originally a long S, which was the old symbol for " sum of" (to-day it is usual to employ the Greek Σ instead). Integration was looked upon as summation. dy being the limit of Δy, and Δy being a small part of y, the differential dy was conceived of as an infinitesimal part of y. An infinite number of dy's were thought of as making up the y.

77. As $d(x^3) = 3\,x^2\,dx$, it follows that

$$\int 3\,x^2\,dx = x^3.$$

But $$d(x^3 + 5) = 3\,x^2\,dx\,;$$

hence $$\int 3\,x^2\,dx = x^3 + 5\,;$$

that is, the integral of $3\,x^2\,dx$ (or the primitive of $3\,x^2$) may be x^3 or $x^3 + 5$, and evidently also $x^3 + 17$ or $x^3 + $ *any constant whatever.* In general, $\int F'(x)dx$ is $F(x) + C$, where C is any arbitrary constant. For the latter expression differentiated gives the former (§ 27).

An arbitrary constant (usually denoted by C) must therefore always be supplied after integrating any differential to obtain the complete integral.

78. There is no general method of integration known corresponding to the general method of differentiation of Chapter I. The only way we arrive at the primitive of a given function is through our previous knowledge of what function differentiated will yield the given function.

79.
$$\int ax^n dx = \frac{ax^{n+1}}{n+1} + C,$$

provided n is not $= -1$. For the differential of $\dfrac{ax^{n+1}}{n+1} + C$ is evidently $ax^n dx$ provided $n+1$ is not zero ; *i.e.* provided n is not $= -1$.

The rule, therefore, for integrating the simplest algebraic function is to increase the exponent by one, and divide the coefficient by the exponent so increased (and then, of course, to add an arbitrary constant).

Thus, $\qquad \int 2\,x^2\,dx$ is $\frac{2}{3}\,x^3 + C.$

80. EXAMPLES.

$$\int 2\,x\,dx = ?$$

$$\int 5\,x^4\,dx = ?$$

$$\int 3\,x^5\,dx = ? \qquad \textit{Ans.} \ \ \tfrac{1}{2}x^6 + C.$$

$$\int \frac{x\,dx}{2} = ?$$

$$\int x^{-2}\,dx = ?$$

$$\int \frac{dx}{x^3} = ? \qquad \textit{Ans.} \ \ -\frac{1}{2\,x^2} + C.$$

$$\int \frac{4\,dx}{x^4} = ?$$

81. It may seem at first that a result involving an arbitrary constant can be of little use. But this is far from true. Though we cannot determine the arbitrary constant from the given differential, we may have, in any particular problem, information from some other source which will enable us to determine it, and often, as we shall see, we do not need to determine it at all. We may interpret the constant C geometrically by plotting the equation $y = F(x) + C$. To know $F'(x)dx$ or $F'(x)$ is to know the slope of the curve for any value of x. But evidently the slope of the curve does not determine the curve; since, if the curve were shoved up or down without change of form, it would have just the same slope for the same value of x. The constant C has to do with the vertical position of the curve. It has nothing to do with its form. ·

82. We may profitably follow the plan adopted in introducing the differential calculus, and begin by considering a mechanical and a geometrical application.

We have seen that, knowing a body falls according to the law
$$s = 16\,t^2, \tag{1}$$

we can show that its velocity at any point is
$$\frac{ds}{dt} = 32\,t. \tag{2}$$

Suppose, however, we only know that a body acquired velocity according to law (2), can we pass back to law (1)? As has been said, in the integral calculus it is customary to use the differential form to start with. Accordingly, we write (2) in the form
$$ds = 32\,t\,dt.$$
Integrating, we have
$$s = \int 32\,t\,dt = \frac{32\,t^2}{2} + C = 16\,t^2 + C. \tag{3}$$

Now, although equation (2) with which we started does not enable us to judge of the value of C, we may evaluate C from outside data.

Thus if we know that s is measured from the point at which the body started to fall, we know that when t was zero, s must have been zero too.

Putting $s = 0$ and $t = 0$ in (3), we have

$$0 = 0 + C,$$

or
$$C = 0.$$

After substituting this value of C in (3), the equation takes the definite form

$$s = 16\, t^2.$$

83. Of course, C is not always zero. In fact, in the above example, we might reckon the distance s of the falling body not from the point where it started, but from a point 27 feet above. We then know that when

$$t = 0,\ s = 27.$$

Substituting in (3), we have

$$27 = 0 + C \text{ or } C = 27,$$

and (3) now becomes
$$s = 16\, t^2 + 27.$$

Evidently the value of C depends solely on what origin we use to measure s from.

84. Similarly, if we know the relation between the slope of a curve $\dfrac{dy}{dx}$ and its abscissa, we can obtain the equation of the curve, except for an arbitrary constant which regulates the vertical position of the curve. This example is the true inverse of the geometrical illustration in the differential calculus (§ 12). But for the purpose of the integral calculus we prefer another geometrical example.

85. Suppose we have (Fig. 10) a plot of $y = f(x)$. Give to x an increment Δx, viz. AE or BK, and consider the resulting increment not of y, but of the area $OABC$ or z.

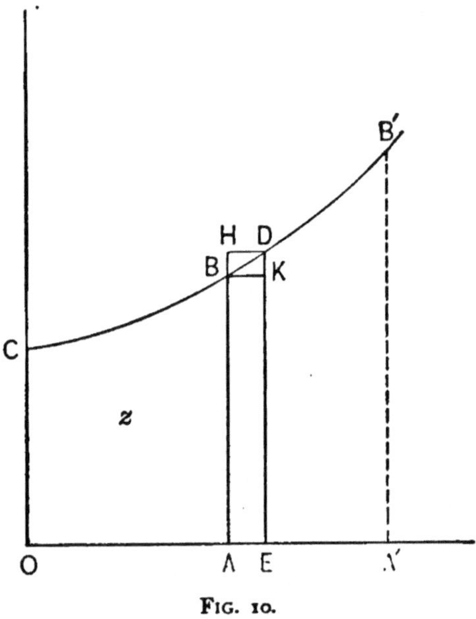

FIG. 10.

This increment Δz of the area is evidently the small area $ABDE$. This small area is the sum of the rectangle $ABKE$ and the tiny triangle BDK. The area of the rectangle is the product of its base Δx by its altitude $f(x)$. So that

$$\Delta z = f(x)\, \Delta x + BDK. \tag{1}$$

Evidently the smaller we make Δx, the smaller the area of BDK becomes relatively to the small rectangle, and may finally be neglected, giving the important equation

$$dz = f(x)dx. \tag{2}$$

This is not, of course, a mere approximation. It is absolutely exact.

The reasoning just given is to be understood as an elliptical form of the following:

Dividing (1) by Δx, we have

$$\frac{\Delta z}{\Delta x} = f(x) + \frac{BDK}{\Delta x}. \tag{3}$$

Now $\dfrac{BDK}{\Delta x}$ is less than

$$\frac{\text{rect } HK}{\Delta x}; \ i.e. \ \frac{\text{rect } HK}{BK}.$$

But the area of a rectangle divided by its base is its altitude — in this case DK. Hence (3) may be written

$$\frac{\Delta z}{\Delta x} = f(x) + \text{ something less than } DK.$$

It is evident that when Δx becomes zero, DK becomes zero, and "something less than DK becomes zero," so that our equation becomes

$$\frac{dz}{dx} = f(x),$$

which may be written

$$dz = f(x)dx.$$

This equation is often written

$$dz = y \, dx, \text{ or } z = \int y \, dx,$$

y being the usual symbol for $f(x)$, the ordinate of a curve.

86. Suppose y or $f(x)$ to be

$$3x^2 + 5;$$

that is, let $y = 3x^2 + 5$ be the equation of a curve. The integral calculus enables us to obtain the area z in terms of the abscissa x.

We know that
$$dz = (3x^2 + 5)\,dx,$$

$$z = \int (3x^2 + 5)\,dx,$$

$$z = x^3 + 5x + C. \tag{1}$$

The student may test the correctness of this integral by differentiating it and obtaining $(3x^2 + 5)dx$.

It remains to determine C. Since we intended to measure the area z from the y-axis, evidently z vanishes when x vanishes. Putting x and z both equal to zero in (1), we obtain $C = 0$. (If we had measured area from some other vertical than the y-axis, the value of C would be different.) Hence (1) becomes $z = x^3 + 5x$.

Thus suppose $x = 3$; then $z = 42$. That is, the area included between the curve $y = 3x^2 + 5$, the axes of coördinates and a vertical 3 units from the y-axis is 42 units. If the linear units be inches, the area units are square inches.

87. We see more clearly now than in § 76 why integration was first conceived of as summation. The area z is evidently the sum of a great many Δz's, and at the limit is conceived of as the sum of an indefinite number of dz's.

The dz is *thought of* as an elementary strip of area infinitely narrow —the limit of $ABDE$.

88. The problem of obtaining curvilinear areas was one of the earliest and is one of the most important of the applications of the integral calculus. Previous to the discovery of this branch of mathematies only a very few curves, such as the circle and parabola, could be so treated.

89. We are here chiefly interested in the geometrical symbolism. We have seen that the *slope* of a curve is the differential quotient of its ordinate (with respect to its abscissa). We now see that the *ordinate* in turn is the differential quotient of its area (also with respect to the abscissa). For $dz = ydx$ means simply

$$\frac{dz}{dx} = y.$$

If we wish to make a graphic picture of any function and its derivative, we can represent the function either by the ordinate *y* of a curve or by its area, while its derivative will then be represented by its slope or ordinate respectively.

If we are most interested in the *function*, we usually employ the former method (in which the ordinate represents the function) ; if in its *derivative*, the latter (in which the ordinate represents the derivative).   That is, we usually like to use the *ordinate* to represent the main variable under consideration.

Jevons in his *Theory of Political Economy* used the abscissa *x* to represent commodity, and the area *z* to represent its total utility, so that its ordinate *y* represented "marginal utility" (*i.e.* the differential quotient of total utility with reference to commodity).   Auspitz and Lieben, on the other hand, in their *Untersuchungen über die Theorie des Preises*, represent total utility by the ordinate and marginal utility by the *slope* of their curve.

90. The method of integration enables us not only to obtain the particular curvilinear area described, but also an area between two limits, as AB and $A'B'$ (Fig. 10).   Evidently this area is the difference of two areas $OA'B'C$ and $OABC$.   The first is the value of $\int f(x)dx$, when OA' (or x_2) is put for x in the integral when found, while the second is the value of the same integral for $x = OA$ (or x_1).   This is expressed as follows :

$$\int_{x=x_1}^{x=x_2} f(x)dx,$$

and is called an *integral between limits*, or a *definite integral.* The reason it is called definite is that it contains no arbitrary constant, for this constant disappears when one of the two integrals concerned is subtracted from the other.

Thus, if $$\int f(x)dx \text{ be } F(x)+C,$$

$$\int_{x=x_1}^{x=x_2} f(x)dx$$

means simply $\quad (F(x_2)+C)-(F(x_1)+C),$

which reduces to $F(x_2)-F(x_1)$, for C must be taken to be the same in both integrals.

The area between the curve $3x^2 + 5$, the x axis, and the two verticals erected at $x = 2$ and $x = 4$ is

$$\int_{x=2}^{x=4} (3x^2 + 5)dx = [x^3 + 5x + C]_{x=4} - [x^3 + 5x + C]_{x=2} = 66,$$

for the C drops out, since for each expression the area is measured from the same vertical, though no matter *what* vertical.

It is usual to abbreviate the expression for limits.

Thus, instead of $\displaystyle\int_{x=2}^{x=4} f(x)dx$, we write $\displaystyle\int_{2}^{4} f(x)dx.$

91. There are certain general theorems of integration corresponding to the general theorems of differentiation of Chapter II. Of these the two most important are :

$$\int Kf(x)dx = K\int f(x)dx$$

and $\quad\displaystyle\int [f_1(x) \pm f_2(x) \pm \cdots)]dx$

$$= \int f_1(x)dx \pm \int f_2(x)dx \pm \int f_3(x)dx \pm \cdots.$$

The proof of the first is simple, for the integral of the right side of the proposed equation is $K(F(x)+C)$, or $KF(x)+KC$ or $KF(x)+C'$, where $F(x)$ means the primitive of $f(x)$ and C is an arbitrary constant. But C' might as well be written C, since its value is anything we please.

The integral on the left is also $KF(x) + C$; for this differentiated gives $Kf(x)dx$.

The proof of the second is also simple. If we denote the primitives of $f_1(x)$, $f_2(x)$, $\cdots$, by $F_1(x)$, $F_2(x)$, $\cdots$, it is evident that the integral on the right is

$$F_1(x) + C_1 \pm F_2(x) + C_2 \pm F_3(x) + C_3 \pm \cdots,$$

or $$F_1(x) \pm F_2(x) \pm \cdots + C, \tag{1}$$

where C is $C_1 + C_2 + C_3$, and is therefore arbitrary. The integral on the left is the same quantity (1), for the differential of (1) is (§ 26),

$$d(F_1(x) \pm F_2(x) \cdots + C) = dF_1(x) \pm dF_2(x) \cdots$$
$$= f_1(x)dx \pm f_2(x)dx \cdots = (f_1(x) \pm f_2(x) \cdots)dx.$$

92. EXAMPLES.

1. Integrate $(1 + a + b)x^2\, dx$.

2. Integrate $x^2\, dx + 7\, x^3\, dx + 5\, x^5\, dx$.

3. Integrate $(h + 2)\{cx^4\, dx + kx^3\, dx\}$.

$$Ans.\ (h + 2)\left\{\frac{c}{5}x^5 + \frac{k}{7}x^7 + C\right\}.$$

4. If the velocity of a body increases with the time according to the formula $\dfrac{ds}{dt} = 3\,t^2$, find the formula for the distance traversed.

5. How far does it move between the instant when t is 3 seconds and that when t is 5 seconds?

6. Find the expression for the area (corresponding to z in Fig. 10) for the curve whose equation is $y = 5\,x^2 + 2$. $Ans.\ \dfrac{5\,x^3}{3} + 2\,x + C.$

7. What is the value of that area for the point where x is 1? Where x is 3? Where y is 22?

8. What is the area between the curve, the x-axis, and the two verticals erected at $x = 2$ and $x = 4$? $Ans.$ 100.

9. Solve the same problems for the curve $y = x^3 + 14$; for $y = x^2$; for $y^2 = 4\,ax$.

10. Find the area z, for $y = a^x$; $y = \log (x + 5)$; $y = \sin x$.
a^x

93. Just as we may differentiate successively, so we may integrate successively.

If we perform the integration

$$\int f(x)dx \quad \text{and obtain} \quad f_1(x),$$

we may then take

$$\int f_1(x)dx \quad \text{and obtain} \quad f_2(x),$$

and then $\qquad \int f_2(x)dx \quad \text{and obtain} \quad f_3(x),$

$$\text{etc.} \qquad\qquad\qquad \text{etc.}$$

Instead of writing $\int f_1(x)dx$, we may substitute for $f_1(x)$ its value $\int f(x)dx$, and we shall have

$$\int \left[\int f(x)dx \right] dx,$$

which, however, is usually abbreviated to $\int \int f(x)dx\, dx$, or even to $\int \int f(x)dx^2$.

Similarly, we may write

$$\int \int \int f(x)\, dx\, dx\, dx, \text{ or } \int \int \int f(x)\, dx^3, \text{ etc.}$$

We may express the double, triple, etc., definite integrals also. The full form for the double definite integral would be

$$\int_{x=a}^{x=b} \left[\int_{x=h}^{x=k} f(x)dx \right] dx \, ;$$

which, however, may be condensed to

$$\int_a^b \int_h^k f(x)\, dx^2.$$

94. To apply these ideas we recur to our old example of a falling body. Suppose our first knowledge is not $s = 16\,t^2$ nor $\frac{ds}{dt} = 32\,t$, but $\frac{d^2s}{dt^2} = 32$; that is, we simply know that the acceleration is a given constant (32 velos per sec.), or to be more general let us call this constant g.

The given equation, $\frac{d^2s}{dt^2} = g$, means, as we know, $\dfrac{d\left(\frac{ds}{dt}\right)}{dt} = g$, or

$$d\left(\frac{ds}{dt}\right) = g\,dt,$$

whence, integrating, $\qquad \dfrac{ds}{dt} = gt + C;$ $\qquad\qquad\qquad$ (1)

but this may be written $\qquad ds = gt\,dt + C\,dt,$

whence, integrating again, $\qquad s = \tfrac{1}{2}gt^2 + Ct + K.$ $\qquad\qquad$ (2)

We have still to determine the arbitrary constants C and K. If the distance s is measured from the starting-point, then s and t vanish simultaneously. Substituting zero for them both in (2), we obtain

$$K = 0.$$

It remains to determine C.

To do this we take equation (1) and suppose the body falls, not from rest, but with an initial velocity of u feet per second; then when t is zero, $\dfrac{ds}{dt}$ is u,

and (1) then reduces to

$$u = 0 + C \quad \text{or} \quad C = u.$$

Substituting $C = u$ and $K = 0$ in equation (2), we have

$$s = \tfrac{1}{2}gt^2 + ut,$$

the general equation of falling bodies.

95. The process which we have followed out in detail from the equation

$$\frac{d^2s}{dt^2} = g$$

may be condensed as follows:

$$s = \int\int d^2s = \int\int g\,dt^2,$$
$$= \int (gt + C)\,dt$$
$$= \tfrac{1}{2}gt^2 + Ct + K.$$

96. The simple transcendental integrals are obtained as follows :

Since $\quad d(\sin x) = \cos x \, dx$, then $\int \cos x \, dx = \mathrm{siu}\, x + C.$

Since $d(\cos x) = -\sin x \, dx$, then $\int -\sin x \, dx = \cos x + C,$

whence $\qquad \int \sin (x) dx = -\cos x - C = -\cos x + C,$

for C is perfectly arbitrary.

Since $\quad d(a^x) = \dfrac{a^x \operatorname{Log} a \, dx}{\operatorname{Log} e}$, then $\int \dfrac{a^x \operatorname{Log} a \, dx}{\operatorname{Log} e} = a^x + C,$

whence $\qquad \int a^x \, dx = \dfrac{a^x \operatorname{Log} e}{\operatorname{Log} a} + C.$

Also, $\qquad \int a^x \, dx = \dfrac{a^x}{\log a} + C.$

Since $d \operatorname{arc\,sin} x = \dfrac{dx}{\sqrt{1 - x^2}}$, then $\int \dfrac{dx}{\sqrt{1 - x^2}} = \operatorname{arc\,sin} x + C.$

Since $\quad d \operatorname{arc\,tan} x = \dfrac{dx}{1 + x^2}$, then $\int \dfrac{dx}{1 + x^2} = \operatorname{arc\,tan} x + C.$

Since $\qquad d \log x = \dfrac{dx}{x}$, then $\int \dfrac{dx}{x} = \log x + C$

$$= \log x + \log K = \log (Kx)$$

ιor C and K are wholly arbitrary.

97. We may summarize the formulæ for integration which have been given :

$$\int a \, dx = ax + C,$$

$$\int a x^n \, dx = \frac{a x^{n+1}}{n + 1} + C \ \text{(when } n \text{ is not} = -1\text{)},$$

$$\int a x^{-1} \, dx = a \log x + C,$$

$$\int k a^x \, dx = \frac{k a^x \operatorname{Log} e}{\operatorname{Log} a} + C$$

$$= \frac{k a^x}{\log a} + C,$$

$$\int e^x\,dx = e^x + C,$$

$$\int \frac{dx}{1 + x^2} = \text{arc tan } x + C,$$

$$\int \frac{dx}{\sqrt{1 - x^2}} = \text{arc sin } x + C,$$

$$\int \sin x\,dx = -\cos x + C,$$

$$\int \cos x\,dx = \sin x + C.$$

98. Treatises on the integral calculus are usually ery bulky, be cause they are occupied with the determination of special integrals, both definite and indefinite, and with special devices for obtaining them. In this little book, which is devoted to only the most general and fundamental principles, we may fitly close our discussion at this point. Practically, even advanced students of the Calculus usually depend on tables of integrals. The reader is referred to B. O. Pierce's "Short Table of Integrals." Completer tables occupy large quarto volumes. An absolutely complete table does not exist, for there are multitudes of integrals which have never yet been solved.

99. We may, however, point out one tool for integrating already in the reader's possession.

Suppose we have to integrate

$$x(x^2 + 2)^3 dx.$$

This may evidently be put in the form

$$(x^2 + 2)^3 x\,dx,$$

or
$$\tfrac{1}{2}(x^2 + 2)^3\, 2\,x\,dx,$$

or
$$\tfrac{1}{2}(x^2 + 2)^3 d(x^2),$$

or
$$\tfrac{1}{2}(x^2 + 2)^3 d(x^2 + 2),$$

and in this form it is easily integrated.

For, putting $u = x^2 + 2$, we have

$$\tfrac{1}{2} u^3 \, du,$$

the integral of which is

$$\frac{u^4}{8} + C,$$

or

$$\frac{(x^2 + 2)^4}{8} + C.$$

This device consists in *changing the variable*, getting rid of dx, and obtaining instead a differential of some other variable, u, in terms of which the whole expression may be written.

100. EXAMPLES.

1. $\int x^{\frac{1}{2}} \, dx = ?$

2. $\int \sqrt[3]{x} \, dx = ?$

3. $\int \frac{a \, dx}{x^3} = ?$ *Ans.* $-\dfrac{a}{2 x^2}.$

4. $\int \frac{dx}{(a - x)^5} = ?$

5. $\int \frac{4 x \, dx}{(1 - x^2)^2}.$

6. $\int \frac{x^8 \, dx}{\sqrt{a^9 + bx^9}}.$

  Ans. $\dfrac{2}{9 b} \sqrt{a^9 + bx^9}.$

7. $\int \frac{dx}{a + x}.$

8. $\int \frac{2 \, bx \, dx}{a - bx^2}.$

9. $\int (a + 3 x^2)^3 \, dx.$

  Ans. $a^3 x + 3 a^2 x^3 + \dfrac{27 \, a}{5} x^5 + \dfrac{27}{7} x^7$

10. $\int \frac{-2 \, dx}{\sqrt{4 - x^2}}.$

APPENDIX

FUNCTIONS OF MORE THAN ONE VARIABLE

101. We have had to do hitherto with functions of only one variable, such as $x^2 + 2x + 3$. But the magnitude $x^2 + 2xy + 3y^2$, for instance, is dependent for its value on *two* variables, x and y; *i.e.* is a function of x and y.

The relation $z = x^2 + 2xy + 3y^2$, or, more generally, $z = F(x, y)$, states that z is a function of x and y; that is, that a change either in x or y produces a change in z.

Thus, the speed of a sailing vessel is a function of the strength of the wind and the angle at which she sails to the wind.

The force which produces tides is a function of the earth's distance from the moon and its distance from the sun.

The price of stocks is a function of the rate of dividends and of the rate of interest.

Similarly, $w = F(x, y, z)$ expresses the fact that w depends on x, y, and z, and so on for any number of variables.

Thus, the force which guides the moon is a function of its distance from the earth, its distance from the sun, and the angle between the directions of these two distances.

The price of a Turkish rug is a function of the prices of its constituents, the cost of transportation, the rate of tariff, etc.

If for $w = F(x, y, z)$, the condition of some special problem should require z to remain constant, the function may be written as $w = \phi(x, y)$; and if y is also constant, as $w = \psi(x)$.

Thus, the speed of a sailing vessel is a function of her angle to the wind, if the strength of the wind remain constant.

The price of woollen cloth is a function of the price of wool, if the cost of labor, etc., remain constant.

102. Since the terms of an equation can be transposed, it is always possible to gather them all on the left side, thus reducing the right side to zero. $y = \sqrt{x^2 + 1}$ is the same equation as $y^2 - x^2 - 1 = 0$. The left member is here a function of x and y. And in general it is evident that any relation between two variables $y = F(x)$ can be reduced to the form $\phi(x, y) = 0$. When expressed in the first form, y is called an *explicit* function of x. In the latter it is an *implicit* function of x.

In like manner, any relation $z = F(x, y)$ can be reduced to the form $\phi(x, y, z) = 0$; any relation $w = F(x, y, z)$ to $\phi(x, y, z, w) = 0$, and so on.

103. We have seen that $\phi(x, y) = 0$ or $y = F(x)$ can always be represented by a curve with x and y as the two coördinates. So, also, $\phi(x, y, z) = 0$ or $z = F(x, y)$ can always be represented by a *surface* with x, y, and z as the *three* coördinates.

Draw three axes at right angles to each other, such as the three edges of a room, meeting at a corner on the floor, the x-axis being directed, say, easterly, the y-axis northerly, and the z-axis upward.

To represent $$z = x^2 + 2xy + 3y^2,$$

let x have any particular value, such as 2, and y, 1.

Then $$z = 2^2 + 2 \times 2 \times 1 + 3 \times 1^2 = 11.$$

Find the point in the room which is 2 units east of the corner, 1 unit north of it, and 11 units above it. This is one point of the required surface. By taking all possible combinations of values of x and y, and finding the resulting values of z, we can find *all* points on the surface.

104. When $z = F(x, y)$, we may vary x by Δx, *while y remains constant*, and thus cause in z an increment denoted by Δz. The ultimate ratio of Δz to Δx is expressed by

$$\frac{\partial z}{\partial x} \text{ or } \frac{\partial F(x, y)}{\partial x},$$

and is called the *partial derivative* of $F(x, y)$ with respect to x.

Similarly, $\qquad \dfrac{\partial z}{\partial y} \text{ or } \dfrac{\partial F(x, y)}{\partial y}$

is the partial derivative with respect to y; *i.e.* the derivative obtained by keeping x constant during the differentiation.

Observe that the symbol ∂, denoting *partial* differentiation, is not identical with d.

105. The geometrical interpretation of these partial derivatives can be made evident. If on the surface, $z = F(x, y)$, say the surface of a stiff felt hat, we take any given point P and pass through it a vertical east and west plane, the plane and surface intersect in a curve passing through P. The tangential slope of this curve at P (or, as we may call it, the E–W slope of the surface itself) is $\dfrac{\partial z}{\partial x}$. For the coördinates of P are x, y, z, and those of a neighboring point Q on the curve (and therefore on the surface) are $x + \Delta x$, y, $z + \Delta z$, where Δx is the difference between the x's of P and Q, and Δz the difference between the z's; the y's are by hypothesis the same. The slope of the line joining P and Q is

$\dfrac{\Delta z}{\Delta x}$, and its limiting value, $\lim \dfrac{\Delta z}{\Delta x}$ or $\dfrac{\partial z}{\partial x}$, is the slope of the curve at P (see § 12); *i.e.* the E–W slope of the surface.

Similarly, $\dfrac{\partial z}{\partial y}$, or $\dfrac{\partial F(x,\,y)}{\partial y}$, is the north and south slope of the surface.

These two *primary slopes* of the surface can be represented by placing two straight wires or knitting needles tangent to the hat at the point P, one in an E–W vertical plane and the other in a N–S vertical plane.

If we take *any* neighboring point R on the surface, its coördinates are $x + \Delta x$, $y + \Delta y$, $z + \Delta z$, where the Δ's are the differences of coördinates of P and R.

Join P and R. Then $\dfrac{\Delta z}{\Delta x}$ represents, not the true slope of the line PR, but its *east and west* slope (not, of course, the east and west slope of the surface itself). It is the rate the line ascends in comparison, not with its true horizontal progress, but with its *eastward* progress. A climber ascending a northeasterly ridge may be rising 5 feet for every 3 of horizontal progress, but yet rising 5 feet for every 2 of eastward progress. We have to do with the latter rate, not the former.

So also $\dfrac{\Delta z}{\Delta y}$ is the *north and south* slope of the same line PR.

Now let R approach P (along *any route whatever* upon the surface) until it coincides. The line PR approaches a limiting position which is a new tangent to the surface (a tangent to that curve in the surface which R traced in approaching P). The E–W slope of this tangent is $\lim \dfrac{\Delta z}{\Delta x}$, called $\dfrac{dz}{dx}$, and its N–S slope, $\dfrac{dz}{dy}$.

Representing this tangent by a third wire, we have three

tangent wires through P, one in an E–W vertical plane, a second in a N–S vertical plane, and the third, *any other* tangent. The first has no N–S slope; its E–W slope is $\frac{\partial z}{\partial x}$. The second has no E–W slope; its N–S slope is $\frac{\partial z}{\partial y}$. The third has both kinds of slope, viz., $\frac{dz}{dx}$ and $\frac{dz}{dy}$.

106. As will be shown, the relation between these various derivatives is

$$dz = \frac{\partial z}{\partial x}\, dx + \frac{\partial z}{\partial y}\, dy, \tag{1}$$

which may be thrown into the forms:

or

$$\left.\begin{aligned} \frac{dz}{dx} &= \frac{\partial z}{\partial x} + \frac{\partial z}{\partial y}\cdot\frac{dy}{dx} \\[2ex] \frac{dz}{dy} &= \frac{\partial z}{\partial x}\cdot\frac{dx}{dy} + \frac{\partial z}{\partial y} \end{aligned}\right\}. \tag{2}$$

The form (1) has the great advantage of symmetry. It seems, however, to conceal the existence of $\frac{dy}{dx}$ or $\frac{dx}{dy}$, which are brought out in (2). These last two magnitudes require merely a word of explanation. $\frac{dy}{dx}$ is not an upward slope at all, as it does not involve the vertical z. It is the inclination of the third wire across the floor, the rate at which a moving point on it proceeds north in relation to its eastward progress.

107. The proof of the formula stated in the last section is as follows : *

* In order to master and remember this proof, the student is advised to construct for it some actual physical model. He will then find it extremely simple.

We first assume that all wires through P tangent to the surface lie in one and the same plane called the *tangent plane*. This assumption is analogous to that in § 14, that the progressive and regressive tangents coincide. There is an exception if the surface has an edge or wrinkle at the given point.

Let us take in this plane the three tangent wires above considered, viz. the two primary wires (in vertical planes running E–W and N–S respectively) and the wire obtained as the limiting position of PQ. Take a point Q' on this third or "general" wire, having coördinates $x + \Delta'x$, $y + \Delta'y$, $z + \Delta'z$. (The primes serve to distinguish Q' on the tangent plane from Q on the surface.)

Through Q' pass two vertical planes running E–W and N–S respectively. We already have two such planes through P. These four vertical planes cut the tangent plane in a parallelogram, of which PQ' is a diagonal and the "primary wires" are the two sides meeting at P. Denote the two vertices as yet unlettered by H and K, the former being in the E–W and the latter in the N–S primary wire.

$\Delta'z$ being the difference in level of P and Q' is the sum of the difference in level of P and H and of H and Q', just as the difference in level between Mount Blanc and the sea is the sum of the elevation of Lake Lucerne above the sea and of Mount Blanc above the Lake. (It does not matter whether H is or is not intermediate in level between P and Q', for if not, one of the heights considered becomes negative.)

Now the difference in level of P and H is

$$\frac{\partial z}{\partial x}\,\Delta'x,$$

for the difference of level, h, between any two points, as M and N

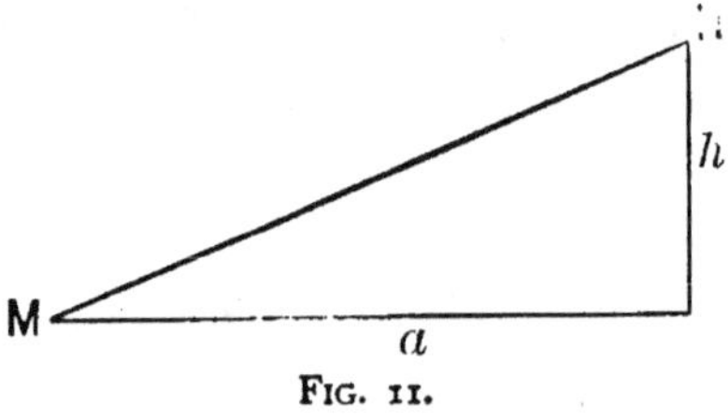

FIG. 11.

(Fig. 11) is the product of the slope of MN by the horizontal interval, a, between them (since: slope of $MN = \dfrac{h}{a}$, whence $h = a \times$ slope of

MN). $\dfrac{\partial z}{\partial x}$ is known to be the slope of PQ', and $\Delta'x$ is the E–W interval between P and Q', and therefore also the E–W interval (or in this case the horizontal interval) between P and H (since H and Q' are in the same N–S plane).

Again the difference in level between H and Q' is

$$\frac{\partial z}{\partial y}\,\Delta'y.$$

For $\dfrac{\partial z}{\partial y}$, being the slope of PK, is also the slope of HQ' parallel to PK, and $\Delta'y$, being the N–S interval between P and Q', is also the N–S (and in this case horizontal) interval between H and Q' (since H and P are in the same E–W plane).

Therefore,

$$\Delta'z = \frac{\partial z}{\partial x}\,\Delta'x + \frac{\partial z}{\partial y}\,\Delta'y. \tag{1$'$}$$

which is the prototype of the desired result **(1)**.

This may be written $\quad\dfrac{\Delta'z}{\Delta'x} = \dfrac{\partial z}{\partial x} + \dfrac{\partial z}{\partial y}\cdot\dfrac{\Delta'y}{\Delta'x}.$ \hfill (2$'$)

Now $\dfrac{\Delta'z}{\Delta'x}$ is the E–W slope of the "general tangent" wire PQ'. But we have seen that $\dfrac{dz}{dx}$ is also this slope. Again, $\dfrac{\Delta'y}{\Delta'x}$ is the inclination of this same wire across the floor (the rate at which a point moving on the wire proceeds *northward* relatively to its *eastward* progress). But so also is $\dfrac{dy}{dx}$ (§ 106). Substituting therefore these values for the primed expressions, we have

$$\frac{dz}{dx} = \frac{\partial z}{\partial x} + \frac{\partial z}{\partial y}\cdot\frac{dy}{dx},$$

which may be thrown into the form

$$dz = \frac{\partial z}{\partial x}\,dx + \frac{\partial z}{\partial y}\,dy.$$

In this, dz is called the *total differential* of z, while $\dfrac{\partial z}{\partial x}\,dx$ and $\dfrac{\partial z}{\partial y}\,dy$ are its *partial differentials*.

It is evident that we should reach the same result if in the preceding reasoning we had employed K in the way we did employ H, and *vice versa;* also that we could have divided $(1)'$ by $\Delta'y$ instead of by $\Delta'x$.

108. The formula (1) ($\S$ 106), or its two alternative forms (2), enable us to ascertain the direction of *any* tangent line to a surface.

Thus, let the surface be

$$z = x^2 + 2\,xy + 3\,y^2,$$

and let it be required to determine any tangent line at the point whose x and y are 1 and 1 respectively; z is evidently 6.

1. The primary E–W tangent wire at this point has an E–W slope $\frac{\partial z}{\partial x} = 2\,x + 2\,y = 4$, found by differentiating the above equation treating y as constant, and has no N–S slope.

2. The primary N–S tangent wire at this point has a N–S slope $\frac{\partial z}{\partial y} = 2\,x + 6\,y = 8$, and has no E–W slope.

3. The tangent wire in the vertical plane running northeast and southwest has an E–W slope of

$$\frac{dz}{dx} = \frac{\partial z}{\partial x} + \frac{\partial z}{\partial y} \cdot \frac{dy}{dx}$$
$$= 4 + 8\frac{dy}{dx}$$
$$= 4 + 8 \times 1 = 12,$$

and a N–S slope of

$$\frac{dz}{dy} = \frac{\partial z}{\partial x} \cdot \frac{dx}{dy} + \frac{\partial z}{\partial y}$$
$$= 4 \times 1 + 8 = 12.$$

4. The tangent wire in the vertical plane running northwest and southeast has the two slopes

$$4 + 8(-1) = -4$$

and

$$4(-1) + 8 = +4.$$

5. The tangent wire in the vertical plane cutting between north and east so as to be advancing north twice as fast as east

$$\left(i.e.\ \text{so that } \frac{dy}{dx} = 2\right),$$

has slopes of

$$\frac{dz}{dx} = \frac{\partial z}{\partial x} + \frac{\partial z}{\partial y} \cdot \frac{dy}{dx}$$

$$= 4 + 8 \times 2 = 20,$$

and

$$\frac{dz}{dy} = \frac{\partial z}{\partial x} \cdot \frac{dx}{dy} + \frac{\partial z}{\partial y}$$

$$= 4 \times \tfrac{1}{2} + 8 = 10,$$

and so on for any tangent wire whatever.

109. EXAMPLES.

1. Find the slopes of the five sorts above indicated for the same surface at the point for which $x = 3$ and $y = 2$.

2. At the point where $x = -1$, $y = -1$.

3. At the point where $x = 0$, $y = 0$.

4. For the surface $z = x^3 + x^2 + x + xy + y + y^2 + y^3$ at the point $x = 0$, $y = 1$.

5. For the surface

$$z = x^2 y - 2 x^2 y^2 + 3$$

at the point $x = 2$, $y = 3$.

6. On the same surface at the same point, what are the E–W and N–S slopes of the tangent line which progresses northward 3 times as fast as eastward ? 4 times ? $3\tfrac{1}{2}$ times ?

7. Answer the same questions for $z = \log y + 3^x + xy$.

110. When we have a function of more than two variables, as $w = F(x, y, z)$, there is no mode of geometrical interpretation corresponding to the curve for $y = F(x)$ and surface for $z = F(x, y)$ (unless, indeed, we posit a " fourth dimension," and speak of a " curved space " of three dimensions whose coördinates are x, y, z, w !).

It may be shown, however, in a manner strictly analogous to the process of § 107, but without employing the geometrical image, that

$$dw = \frac{\partial w}{\partial x} dx + \frac{\partial w}{\partial y} dy + \frac{\partial w}{\partial z} dz.$$

This differential equation is elliptical for the three equations obtained by dividing through by dx, dy, and dz.

The theorem and its proof are extensible to any number of variables.

111. A very important application of the principle of partial derivatives occurs when we have but two variables, but y is an implicit function of x: *i.e.* when $\phi(x, y) = 0$. We are enabled to obtain the derivative $\frac{dy}{dx}$ without being obliged first to transform the implicit function into the explicit form $y = F(x)$.

Thus, if $x^2 + y^2 = 25$, we may find $\frac{dy}{dx}$ without changing the equation to the form $y = \pm \sqrt{25 - x^2}$.

112. We know from § 106 (2) that if $z = \phi(x, y)$, then

$$\frac{dz}{dx} = \frac{\partial \phi(x, y)}{\partial x} + \frac{\partial \phi(x, y)}{\partial y} \cdot \frac{dy}{dx},$$

which may also be written in two other forms, as given in § 106.

When z is zero, as in the case now being considered, then $\frac{dz}{dx}$ is also zero (§ 27, end). Making this substitution in the above equation, we obtain

$$\frac{dy}{dx} = - \frac{\dfrac{\partial \phi(x, y)}{\partial x}}{\dfrac{\partial \phi(x, y)}{\partial y}}.$$

In words: *To find the differential quotient of y with respect to x when the functional dependence between x and y is expressed in the implicit form $\phi(x, y) = 0$, differentiate the function $\phi(x, y)$ with respect to x, treating y as constant, and then a ain with res ect to   treatin x as constant.*

Take the partial derivative found from the first differentiation, divide it by that found from the second, and prefix the minus sign.

Thus, if $x^2 + y^2 = 25$, or $x^2 + y^2 - 25 = 0$, we may find $\frac{dy}{dx}$ as follows:

The partial derivative of $x^2 + y^2 - 25$ with respect to x is $2x$, and with respect to y, $2y$. Hence

$$\frac{dy}{dx} = -\frac{2x}{2y} = -\frac{x}{y}.$$

This result is expressed in terms of both x and y, but it may be transformed so as to involve but one variable. Thus, substitute for y its value as obtained from $x^2 + y^2 = 25$, viz. $\pm\sqrt{25 - x^2}$. Then

$$\frac{dy}{dx} = -\frac{x}{\pm\sqrt{25 - x^2}},$$

a result identical with that obtained by differentiating the explicit form

$$y = \pm\sqrt{25 - x^2}.$$

113. EXAMPLES.

1. Find $\frac{dy}{dx}$, if $xy = 1$.

2. Find $\frac{dy}{dx}$, if $2x^2 + 3y^2 - 4 = 0$.

3. Find $\frac{dy}{dx}$, if $ax^2y^3 + bx^3y^2 = 0$.

4. Find $\frac{dy}{dx}$, if $\frac{x+y}{x-y} + \frac{bx}{cy} + \frac{h}{k} = 0$.

5. Find $\frac{dy}{dx}$, if $\cos(xy) = x$.

6. Find $\frac{dy}{dx}$, if $\log(x^2y^2) + x^3 + y^1 + 2xy + a = 0$.

7. Show § 112 geometrically.

114. Functions of many variables are peculiarly applicable in economic theory, though as yet they have been very little employed.*   Many fallacies have been committed from lack of this more general conception of functional dependence, and from the tacit assumption that mere *curves* are capable of delineating any sort of quantitative relation. This is an error only one degree less flagrant than the errors of those whose sole mathematical idea is that of the constant quantity.

* See, however, Edgeworth's *Mathematical Psychics*, 1881; the author's *Mathematical Investigations in the Theory of Value and Prices*, 1892; and Pareto's *Cours d'économie politique*, 1896–7.